AF241900

Welcome Home

Chelsea Robillard

"I think that sometimes love gets in the way of itself
- you know, love interrupts itself. We want things so
much that we sabotage them."

- Jack White

1

"Excuse me miss," said the conductor, as I slowly opened my groggy eyes to a middle aged man with a moustache the size of a television remote resting so slick on his upper lip that not even the worst of winds could budge it. I pursed my lips and held in a chuckle for fear of seeming rude, but I assure you, you would have done the same if you opened your eyes to the sight I did. It took me a moment to gather myself and remember where I was, aboard the train headed straight for Corner Brook, Newfoundland. A town that was once home to me. After the shock of being jolted awake by the moustache man, I realized the distinct look of panic in his eyes and the beads of sweat forming just above his brow. Not to mention, the severe lack of passengers that made themselves known earlier with all the hustle and bustle from cart to cart.

"Is there a problem?"

"Well actually ma'am, I'm afraid there is. You see it appears the train has collided with an unbeknownst object that has caused the train to derail itself from the tracks."

"This must be some kind of joke right, or a dream", I thought instantly. "C'mon wake up Beth, wake up wake up wake up!"

"Excuse me, miss, miss," said the conductor to my surprise, this time actually waking me up from a rather vivid dream. Or nightmare. Depends how you want to look at it, really. At least one thing was real, the moustache.

"I don't mean to bother you ma'am, but my shift is ending and I just wanted to see if you wouldn't rather head to your cabin for the night. I do believe it would be much more comfortable."

"Oh that's alright, thanks. I'm good here."

"As you wish," said the conductor. And so I stayed there, nuzzling deeper into the seat as I prepared to spend another night on the train.

***

And that was how the beginning of the rest of my life started. The beginning I never saw coming, never in my wildest dreams imagined to be a possibility .

I guess it just goes to show we really don't have total control on the way we want things to unfold. I'm getting a little bit ahead of myself.

Let me start from the beginning, the train. I recently had a life altering experience that left me no choice but to get packing and head back to the one true place that would always be home. Corner Brook. There was just something about it. Maybe it was the ocean, or the trees. Or maybe, it was the people. Either way, they always say that if you have a good thing set if free, and if it comes back it's yours forever, right? As hard as it was for me to leave Corner Brook all those years ago, I have a feeling it might be even harder for me to return now. Especially under my new circumstances.

I remember the three days I spent on the train from Vancouver really well, almost as if it was just the other day, but its been about six months now. Sometimes I can still hear the jolt of the breaks, smell the freshly made cinnamon buns that tempted me each morning as I made the trek from my cabin across the train to the communal kitchen. I will admit, the cinnamon buns won the fight each time. But above all, I can still see him sitting there, in his cabin, unknowingly taunting me just by being present.

I had had more than enough of staring out the window and fighting the waves of motion sickness that seemed to only show themselves at night. I unwillingly unwrapped myself from the burrito fold I had managed to tangle myself in to with the help of the less than comfortable blankets provided by the train - but who am I to complain. I liked to walk up and down the hallway of the train at night, it was so peaceful with everyone else asleep. Some may think it to be more eerie than comforting, but there was something about the silence that calmed me. It reminded me of the first moment I opened my eyes in the morning and looked over and saw Aiden. For a few moments each morning that's all there was in the world. Just him and me, laying frozen in time as the rest of the world moved around us.

This was my second night on the train, meaning I had one more overnight before I made it home - home it sounds almost weird to say that considering I haven't been back there since I left twelve years ago.

I remember seeing a light on at the very far end of the train, so naturally, I followed it. When I reached the open cabin door, I placed myself in the centre of the doorframe and stopped dead in my tracks.

"Oh - I'm sorry. I didn't mean to disturb you."
"No worries. Would you like to come in?"
There he was. The spitting image of Aiden. I've heard people mention doppelgängers before but I never thought much of it - until now.
"What are you doing up? It's pretty late. I thought I was the only night owl on this train."
"Couldn't sleep."
"Cheers to that. I'm Ben by the way. It's nice to meet you —"
"Oh right. Bethany. Beth. I'm Bethany," I said as I extended my hand to meet his.
"If you don't mind me asking Bethany, is there something on my face?"

I didn't really know how to respond to that so I quickly took a peek at his face and it was full of things.

Aiden's piercing blue eyes, his sandy blonde hair - although Ben wore it much shorter than Aiden ever did, and his smile, the one that crept up only on one side.

"I just mean that when you first showed up in the doorway, you looked at me as though you were seeing a ghost."

"I'm sorry it's not you. Gosh I don't even know you, although I feel like I do. You look exactly like someone I used to know."
"Well I hope they were handsome."

And there it was. He had Aiden's sense of humour too. This was all too good to be true, but that didn't stop me from entertaining it for a few hours. I spent the rest of the night into the early hours of the morning talking with Ben, learning all about him. When we exhausted all of each others questions we headed for the bar and broke in to make ourselves a few drinks - don't worry, we left money in exchange for the drinks we had. But just like every other good thing in life, they must come to an end.

When the sun showed itself and the morning hours arrived, the train began to fill up with all of the other passengers that were bustling about from cart to cart. Just like that Ben was gone back to his cabin and last night was now nothing more than a memo-ry.

Remembering I left my things behind in Ben's cab-in, I retraced my steps and found the door opened just like it had been last night - although this time there was no one in it. Although I had just met him,

I missed him. For a brief period in the late hours of the night on the train, Ben had helped me forget. I found my things where I had left them along with a note that read "It was nice to meet you last night Bethany. Sorry I couldn't catch you on my way out I was the first stop this morning. I'd love to do it again sometime. Maybe after closing hours at a local mall or off season at an amusement park. Take care, Ben." I couldn't help but laugh at the fact he clearly put some thought into finding odd times and places to get to know someone, but I appreciated it. It felt nice.

With my note in hand and blanket slumped over my shoulders, I headed back across the train - past the families sitting down to breakfast , the lone travellers like myself and just as I was about to reach my room, there was moustache man exiting his cabin and getting ready to start his shift.

"Well good morning ma'am. Sleep well?"
"No," I said with a smile. "I didn't sleep much at all." With that, I headed into my own cabin, pulled my sleep mask over my eyes and dozed off. When I woke up, I couldn't believe what I was hearing. It seemed as though I more than caught up on the sleep that I had missed the previous night because

we were pulling into the station in Corner Brook. When I peeked my head outside my cabin I noticed passengers not so patiently waiting to get off and go on with their lives. For the life of me I just sat there - not really sure where I was headed to or what was in store for me. I checked into Corner Brook on my phone, making it official in attempt to let my new reality sink in.

"Is this your first time in Corner Brook?" Asked the conductor who I had gotten to know over the last few days and frankly thought I may even miss a little.
"Not at all. I've been here before."
"Oh well welcome back. I hope you enjoy your stay. What brings you back to town?"
"This is home."

2

I remember my first day back in Corner Brook probably the most vividly of them all. That was the day I met Elizabeth. The moment I got off the train, it felt as though I had never left. So many emotions came flooding back all at once, consuming me entirely. It was short lived when I came back down to earth trying to catch my balance amongst the large crowd headed for the baggage claim. I was so overwhelmed with being back, I almost lost all of my things when I noticed a young woman walking off with my suitcase. I suppose that's what I get for not using one of those luggage name tags.

"Excuse me! Hey? Hello!" I don't know if she was intentionally ignoring me or genuinely didn't realize she was the target of my yelling.
"Me?"
"Yes you. I think you have my stuff."
"No I'm sorry. This is my bag. I'm sure of it."

I walked around her and reached forward, turning the bag on its side - and there it was. "Ah ha see, right there. That big old scratch on the back. I did that when I dropped it down the stairs a few years back."

She handed me the bag, as her cheeks went three shades of red, apologizing countless times. I kind of felt bad for being so forward. We laughed it off and went our separate ways. I offered to wait and help her find her actual luggage since I knew exactly what it looked like, but she insisted that she would be alright. Besides, I was just stalling from the house I had to get to.

I made my way through the twists and turns of the station, until I found an exit that looked promising. I managed to find a taxi and head out to my new home. Upon arriving, I gathered my things from the trunk with the help of the nice man who drove me here. I gave him a tip, turned around and took a deep breath, preparing to walk into my new home for the first time - alone.

I walked through the front door and it was as though I had entered into a time machine. All of the houses here seemed to use the exact same floor plan.

It was kind of nice knowing right off the bat where everything is, but also kind of lonely being back here by myself. If I looked past the emptiness of the place and the damp unkept smell, I could see my family gathered in the kitchen eating breakfast on a Saturday morning. I just stood there for a few moments at a time in each room and pulled at my memories that had been lost in the depths of my mind.

Plenty of time had gone by, but I couldn't bring myself to unpack my things just yet, I thought by doing so it would make everything too real - it later turned out I was right. I spent the better part of that day cooped up in what was meant to be the living room, inside the world that lived within the screen of my phone. You can do everything online nowadays. I ordered dinner and had it delivered, I ordered some furniture that would be arriving in the next couple of weeks - this place was in some desperate need of a makeover. The next thing I did I'm not proud of, but I even went on Facebook and cyber stalked all of my old high school classmates to see if any of them still lived here in town. Turned out a few of them did.

I became so consumed that I missed the sun go down and when I took a breather and looked up, it was pitch black outside and hours had gone by. Hours I would never get back, but I didn't care. I spent the next couple of days like this. Without the courage or the will to leave the house, I found company online and in movies. I was basically living out of my suitcase like someone on vacation, but this was no vacation for me - this was my life.

After a week of takeout and not showering, the dampness wasn't the only unpleasant smell around here. I dragged myself up the stairs and into the shower, feeling visibly refreshed and renewed when I got out. I made my way down the hall to the master bedroom that had yet to be furnished. I turned myself upside down and quickly towel dried my hair before all the blood had the chance to rush into my head. When I stood up I saw him there. Aiden, in the bedroom in one of his ratty old white t-shirts that he always wore around the house when he was getting stuff done. "I only have one or two nice ones" he would always say. "I have to keep them safe so you won't make me go shopping again." I laughed at the memory then watched him work for a little while as he built the bureau I had ordered online last week.

"So how does it look?" He said while posing like a fool in front of the furniture.

"Great," I said and let out a burst of laughter. "It got here faster than I had thought. When did you get home?"

"Wherever you are is home to me. I'm always here."

I smiled at him then I blinked and he was gone. Sometimes I forget.

I went back downstairs to my makeshift living room - a bunch of cushions on the floor lumped together with a few throw blankets and a laundry basket turned bottoms up that acted as a table. I fell back into my new routine of scrolling and cyber stalking. I was beginning to think I could live like this for a while. Only making friends online saved me from the potential loss and heartache of losing them in real life. I can come and go as I wish with no expectations. And that's exactly what I did. I searched #CornerBrook and found local Facebook groups catered to almost anything I could imagine. I joined one that shares healthy recipes to keep everyone on track, one where people share cute animal videos - which I must admit took up a good chunk of my time, along with many others that interested me to keep myself busy. Sometimes it's easier to have friends online who don't know every last detail about who you are. It makes it easier to tell them things. There's less judgement - in my opinion anyways.

Then, late one night when I was feeling particularily low, I typed in support groups and found one for widows right here in Corner Brook. I scrolled through the members and didn't recognize anyone at first glance. I spent some time reading through peoples posts and comments not yet ready to jump in myself as it is still a raw subject for me. I stopped scrolling when I saw that they were holding a meeting the following night just a few blocks from my house - a meeting they hold weekly. I knew I wasn't quite ready for it yet, but I also knew I needed to get out of the house.

The following evening I managed to get myself as presentable as I could which meant jeans and one of Aiden's t-shirts. The nice ones not the ones he wore to do work around the house. If I tied it just right and tucked it into my jeans it was actually kind of cute. One of these days I'll get the strength to donate it to good will - just not yet. It had been days since I had washed my hair so a messy pony tail and a bottle of dry shampoo was what I was working with.

Since the meeting was being held just a few blocks from my house, I decided to walk, it was a nice night. The entire way there I had to talk myself into it because my mind knew it was the right thing to do but my feet just wanted to turn back around and run in the opposite direction. I arrived a little after seven which was when the meeting was set to start. I didn't really want to be there in the first place and now I was late. I could always chicken out and go home, but I didn't. I was looking for more than just support. I was lonely, I was looking for a friend. I did my best to sneak in with no help from the creaky door. I shimmied past a few people standing along the back wall and found a seat off to the side in the back row. It was then that I realized I had interrupted someone's story. It's always the moments when you're trying to be quiet that you're more loud than you've ever been - like when you need a snack but everyone in the house is asleep. I sat on the edge of my chair, in total discomfort, but I didn't dare move for fear of bringing all attention to myself. I remained there until the meeting was over, not offering up any stories of my own just yet.

I felt like the new kid in class who just transferred and let me tell you I wanted nothing more than to go back where I came from. As I was headed out I heard someone call out "Hey. Hey you."

"No No this is not happening," I whispered to my-self under my breath with my head down. I not so smoothly spun around and said "Hi There."
"I couldn't help but notice you come in mid way through my story."
"I know. I'm sorry about that. Trust me I did not mean to be late."
"Oh don't mind him dear," came a voice from an older lady who apparently had been eavesdropping on our conversation. "He's just miserable."
"I am not," said the man.
"And scene," responded the woman as she mo-tioned her hand in front of her face the way actors do in movies.
"Am I missing something?"
The two strangers looked from one another then to me and laughed. I laughed along with them ner-vously not knowing how else to respond.
"Oh we're just messing with you. We do it to all the new comers, ya know, trying to lighten the mood. Also, it's fun for us. I'm Gloria and this is —"

"I'm Ethan."

"Nice to meet you Gloria and Ethan. I'm Bethany."

"Ou what a lovely name," said Gloria as she not so subtly examined me from head to toe - stopping mid way to take in my shirt but deciding against saying whatever she was so clearly thinking.

"Thank you. I don't mean to be rude but I have to get going."

"No worries," hollered Gloria.

"I hope we didn't freak you out," called Ethan, but it was too late I was already out the door and half-way up the block - when it started to rain.

I ran into the closest place I could find that was opened. It was a small coffee shop that must have been built between the time I left and now because I didn't recognize it. I had been a frequent coffee shop girl back in my day so I think I would have remembered. I found a table by the window so I could watch the world go by outside. I watched as cars drove by and people scurried for shelter away from the rain. It's kind of funny if you think about it, the way we get so concerned about getting caught in the rain when all it really is is water - but who am I to judge from inside the warm dry coffee shop I ran into.

I ordered a black coffee and added one cream and one sugar. I hadn't realized anyone new had come in to the cafe, but there she was. It was the girl from the train station. I saw this as my opportunity to make a friend here in town since we had already broken the ice earlier.

"Hey there. Do you remember me?"
"Oh my gosh. Hi. Yeah from the train station. I'm so sorry about that by the way I really did think that was my bag."
"Please don't worry about it. I just wanted to properly introduce myself. My name is Bethany, I'm new to town. That day at the train station was my first day actually."
"No way. Welcome, I'm Elizabeth."

3

You know that moment you meet someone and you just click? You know you're going to be the best of friends right from the start? Well that's how I felt with Elizabeth. I was so afraid that it would be hard to make a friend especially at my age. It's hard enough making new friends in high school, try when you're thirty years old and everyone already has their go to friends, a busy life and in most cases not enough time or will to go out seeking new company. I knew I couldn't let this one slip through my fingers. I hurried home that night after the coffee shop and got straight to work. I googled, facebooked, searched on twitter and even checked if she had a tumblr - but ultimately instagram was where I got all of my answers. You can find out almost anything you want to know about a person from their instagram page. The foods they like, where they like to hang out and with who. Luckily for me, her privacy settings were turned off. From the looks of it, Elizabeth is a frequent flyer at the cafe where I saw her. She doesn't appear to be married and she really likes home decor. Her feed almost looks like a professional blog except for the random selfies here and there - but who doesn't love a good selfie. I could feel myself getting excited the more I scrolled, looking and absorbing all of her memories. I could imagine all of the instagram worthy things we would do together - I couldn't wait.

I didn't really know the proper etiquette for adult friendships, so I waited until the following morning before I said anything. We had exchanged numbers at the cafe out of sheer politeness and just something one does. I bet she never expected anything to come of it, but I on the other hand had a different vision in mind. I paced back and forth in front of the mirror planning out what I would say, even though she wouldn't actually hear anything because I was sending a text message. I quickly typed in "Hey it's Beth, any plans for today" and hit send before I could change my mind. She answered me about twenty minutes later and said she was busy which made me bummed but then added that the rest of her week was open. We went on to make plans to meet back at the coffee shop the following day for lattes and lunch. I rushed up to my room and started rummaging through my suitcase and piles of clothes scattered all around in search of the perfect outfit.

I barely slept that night. I just kept replaying how I hoped our lunch would go over and over in my mind.

We had planned to meet for twelve in the afternoon so at ten to I grabbed my bag and headed out the door. I didn't want to get there too early and seem eager, so I slowed my pace. I arrived at the cafe around five minutes passed and saw Elizabeth waving at me from the other side of the window.

"Hey stranger, long time no see," she said.
"You can say that again."
"So what will it be?"
"Whatever you're having is fine, as long as there are no nuts - I'm allergic."
"Noted," said Elizabeth and walked up to the counter. She came back a few moments later with two iced lattes and a chocolate fudge brownie to share, although I would have had no problem polishing one off on my own.

"So, what brings you to Corner Brook?"
"I'm actually from here. Born and raised."
"Oh get out, what brings you back then?"
"Just life I guess. It was time to come home. What about you. Coming home from an exciting vacation?"

"I wouldn't call it exciting. I was just visiting with my parents for a few weeks. They live out in Vancouver. That's where I'm from. I moved here with them a few years back. They never really got into a routine they liked here - when they headed back I decided to stay. I already had my business up and running at that point anyways."

"Business?"

"I'm an interior designer."

"That's cool."

"Yeah, I think so. I used to flip houses with my husband. He did all of the heavy lifting and I made the place look nice - gave it that homey feel. But it's just me now."

I could tell there was more to the story by the look on her face, but I didn't want to push, especially not this early in our friendship anyways. I didn't want to seem like I was putting my nose where it doesn't belong. I just smiled and shook my head. Elizabeth seemed to catch on to what I was doing, because she reciprocated the smile.

After coffee, she invited me back to her place for some iced tea. I was so worried we would have coffee and call it a day and that would be that. The fact that she was putting effort onto the friendship just made me even more excited and hopeful. Maybe coming home wouldn't be so bad after all. When I got to her house, I followed her through the beautiful french doors and had to pick my jaw up off the perfectly polished floor soon after. If I didn't believe her when she said she was an interior designer, I sure did now. Everything about the place looked like it was carefully chosen right out of a page from a magazine and placed perfectly in the house. It had an open floor plan with white walls as far as the eye can see, which provided amazing lighting by the way. I felt like I was at a resort.

"You did all of this," I asked, motioning my arms wide, making sure to cover the space in its entirety.
"I did. I know it's a lot. Sometimes I get carried away."
"It's — perfect. I wish my place looked like this."
"Well, I could help you. Only if you wanted?"
"Really?"
"Sure. What are friends for, right?"
"Thank you. That would be amazing."

I left shorty after that and walked back home from Elizabeth's. She had offered to drop me off, but she only lived about a fifteen minute walk from me which was a happy coincidence. Besides, I wasn't really ready for anyone to see the way I had been living since I moved in. It was really starting to look like someone had been squatting in there. When I got home, I was in such good spirits about our shopping trip set for the following day that I just cleaned. I cleaned for hours. I started in the living room and made my way throughout the house, making sure not to miss a thing. I wanted it to be perfect - or at least as perfect as I could make it with what I had to work with. I was still waiting on a few of the pieces I had ordered to come in.

I got scared half to death when I reached the bedroom. I had been turned away from the hall, making the bed and when I turned back around, there was Aiden in the doorway. Standing the way he always did with one arm balancing his weight. His arm was placed just high enough that the bottom of his t-shirt lifted slightly, showing off just the right amount of skin to make me blush. I told him all about Elizabeth and how excited I was to have made a new friend so quickly. I only wish he could have met her. I know they would have gotten along great.

***

I almost forgot to eat breakfast the following morning. My mind was focused on shopping and shopping only. I couldn't wait to see what kind of ideas Elizabeth would have for me. I didn't really have anything in mind going in, I wanted to go with the flow and leave things to chance. It was something I was trying to work on lately. I had spent the majority of my life trying to organize everything down to the very last detail. After recent events its become more clear to me that life can be very unpredictable and you can organize and make lists until you're blue in the face - sometimes they still won't unfold the way you had hoped. Just look at Aiden. He never should have had to face the things that he did so soon. It's unfair.

I grabbed a granola bar, threw it in my purse for later and headed out the door. I couldn't help but hear Sophia's voice in my head going on about how a granola bar is not a proper breakfast. Sophia was my college roommate. She still lives back in Vancouver and I miss her everyday. In some ways Elizabeth reminds me of her, maybe that's why I was so set on making sure our friendship happened. Sophia had studied to become a nutritionist but ultimately gave it up to follow her dream to be a yoga instructor. She's awesome. I was never a yoga fan, but she was able to persuade me ever so slightly. It's hard to get a hold of her sometimes with her being so busy and all, but I know I'll always have a friend for life in her as she will in me.

When I pulled myself back from memory lane, Elizabeth was just pulling up outside my place. I had caved and given her my address. She would have to see the inside anyways if she was going to help me decorate. I know she won't judge me considering I just moved in, but after seeing how glamorous her place is I couldn't help but feel a little insecure about mine. Hopefully after today all of that will fade away.

"How do you feel about throw pillows," she asked before I even had the time to get my seatbelt on.
"They're … nice?"
"Great. I was hoping you'd say that. First stop Home Design & Gifts."

We spent hours in that place and when we left I was surprised to see that they were still open for business. I could have swore we bought out the whole store. Money was pretty tight for me at the time having been off work for a few months, but I couldn't say no to Elizabeth so I dipped into our savings and splurged.

"Hardware store next to look at some paint samples?"
"Maybe another day? I'm really beat."
"Of course," said Elizabeth.

We lugged all of our bags back to the car and stuffed it so tight there almost wasn't enough room for us.

"So, do you always go to the cafe so late at night? I could barely sleep after having caffeine in my system that late."
"I'm there that late once a week."
"Oh, okay."
"What about you. I don't mean to be nosy, but you did say it was your first week back in town and you already had big plans?"
"Actually, I was at a support group down the street."
"The one for grieving widows?"
"Yeah, you've heard of it?"
"That's kind of why I was at the cafe."
"I don't understand."
"It's a bit of a long story for right now, but I've been trying to muster up the courage to walk in there for months now and I just can't do it. If I go in then everything is so much more real. It's stupid, I know."
"I'm so sorry I had no idea. It's not stupid at all. I barely got myself in there that night."

We had arrived back at my house and just sat there in the parked car for a moment, not saying a word. I think we were both trying to tip toe around the subject as much as possible since we both knew how painful it could be. Elizabeth helped me unload the car and bring everything inside. As soon as the last bag was in, she was out of sight. I hope I didn't cross a line.

4

I woke up the following morning the same way I had every morning this past week - to the bird who apparently lives right outside my bedroom window. I suppose he wasn't getting the memo that I already had an alarm clock. Once he made himself known, I was up. I could have tried to doze back off but it never works for me. I had almost forgotten about all of the things I had bought yesterday, but was quickly reminded when I basically tripped all the way down the hall trying to avoid the bags. It felt like I was doing one of those car tire obstacle races down my hallway, trying to avoid breaking anything.
I started rummaging through all the bags, taking things out and organizing them into piles to make the decorating process roll smoothly, when I heard a ping sound coming from the living room. I followed it and saw that I had forgot to shut down my laptop last night before when I went up to bed. It was a Facebook message from Ethan.

"Hey Beth. Is it alright if I call you Beth? Anyways is everything okay, you haven't been very active in the group lately."

"Hey Ethan. Sure you can call me Beth. Ha. Thanks for checking in. Everything is fine, just busy with everything."
"No worries. Will Gloria and me be seeing you this week at the meeting?"
"Yeah. See you there."

I had been so overwhelmed I had forgotten completely about the meeting. I barely managed to make it through the first one but I knew I owed it to myself to at least give it a proper try. I could also use the company, and Ethan and Gloria didn't seem so bad. Maybe I would have a whole new little group of friends in no time. I wish Aiden could have seen how much progress I was making so quickly. I think he would have been proud.

I had spent the following few days leading up to the next meeting fairly low key at home. Mostly just puttering around and trying but not succeeding to give the house that homey feel it was lacking. I heard from Elizabeth off and on, but she seemed busy so I left that be for the time being. I did however get a hold of Sophia and made plans for her to come up here and visit sometime in the next two weeks. That was very exciting seeing as I hadn't seen her for the longest time. It would be nice to have someone familiar around even if it would only be for a little while. It will make this house feel more like home.

Before I knew it, a week had gone by and the next meeting was quickly approaching. I must admit, I was kind of excited to see Ethan and Gloria and continue to get to know them, but I really did not want to step foot back into that building. Telling strangers details about your life online is one thing, but in person when they're all right there staring at you is completely different. I made the dreaded walk to the meeting, feeling like I was having some sort of deja vu. That went away when I opened the doors and saw my two new friends waving me over, right in the front. Of all the seats they could have chosen, they had to sit in the front row. I plastered on a smile and waved back as I walked passed a room full of strangers - feeling more and more uncomfortable the further up I got.

"So," said Ethan, "Is tonight the night?"

"The night for what?"

"For you to get up there and tell us your story. For all we know you could just be some weirdo who crashes support groups."

"Ethan," said Gloria "watch yourself. We barely know the girl. Don't go scaring her away."

"That's quite alright. I get it. I'm the mysterious

new girl no one knows."
"So, you gonna get yourself up there tonight?"
"I don't think so. I have a hard time speaking in front of a room of eyes staring me down."
"It's not so bad darling. Watch, let me show you how it's done."

I watched Gloria as she strutted up the steps of the tiny makeshift stage, demanding the attention of everyone in the room and began to tell her story as if it's the one thing in life she was made for. I don't know how she did it, standing up there with so much grace and confidence speaking her truth. I didn't think I would ever be able to do that. Just the thought of being up there sends shivers up my spine.

"Hello all, my name is Gloria, but I think we all know that by now. I know most of you know why I continue to come here every week - other than for the free donuts and coffee, but just in case you don't here it is. I remember the exact moment I saw him, James, standing in the middle of the court yard. I had been away at college for about two months and was beginning to think I was wasting my time. There were no boys worth pursuing, they were all horrible. Until James. He was tall dark and handsome. Not that any of that mattered once I heard the intelligence flowing out of his mouth with each phrase he spoke. And the way that he carried himself with such strength and kindness - he was like no other man I had ever met. I didn't think people like that existed outside of the movies, but they do, or at least they did. We spent all of our time together and it was as though we had never been apart - like my life began the moment I met James and everything that came before was all leading up to that moment. We were the very best of friends. When we met, he was studying to become a math teacher and I a teacher of the arts. We were the perfect balance for one another. I could go on and on about my love for James, but some things I like to save just for the two of us. We were together for sixty two years, in fact it would have been sixty three today if it weren't for his heart attack. James passed away at the age of seventy six which was far too soon if you ask me. Some may say that he lived a good life, but I wanted his life to be great. I wanted him to be able to get every ounce out of it. To get everything he ever wanted and I know for a fact there were some things he never got to do, but that's just the way the cookie crumbles. I love you my sweet James, always and forever."

As Gloria made her way off the stage and back to her seat, there was not a dry eye in the place, including me.

"That was beautiful Gloria."

"Thanks Dear," she said, taking my hand and squeezing it in her own. "You know, it really does do a great deal of good to get up there and tell your story. It's very freeing, but I understand if you don't want to try."

"I'm just not ready."

"Why don't we start a group of our own?"

"What?" Asked Ethan.

"Are your ears blocked? I said let's start our own support group. Would that make it easier for you to open up if it were just us buddies?"

"I think that just might work. That's a great idea Gloria. We can do it at my place?"

"Of course Dear. Ethan if you're so bothered by the idea, stay home," she looked him right in the eyes and stuck out her tongue.

"Oh grow up. I'll be there."

"There's just one thing," I said.

"What is it," they replied to me in unison.

"I have this friend, Elizabeth. I just met her the other day but we've been getting along really well. She said she tries to make it here but hasn't been able to get herself to come. I know there's more to it, but I didn't want to push. I think she could really use —"

"Say no more," said Gloria. "The more the merrier."

I was so happy they were accepting of inviting Elizabeth to join our group. I practically ran out of the meeting and headed straight for the cafe. I hadn't texted her, but I had a hunch she would be there - I was right.

"Hey!"
"Geez. Trying to terrify me?"
"Sorry. No. I have great news."
"What?"
"Remember I told you about those two people I had met last week at support group?"
"Okay."
"Well we decided to start our own group and it's going to be at my house. Just the four of us."
"Four?"
"Yeah. Gloria, Ethan, me and you?"
"I don't know Beth."
"I think it will be nice. C'mon just give it a try. For me?"
"Fine. When is it?"

5

"Hey Elizabeth, are you busy today?"

"Hi. I have to meet with a client at ten and then my schedule is free. Why what's up?"

"The meeting? At my house?"

"Oh right. How could I forget."

"Oh stop it. It'll be good."

"If you say so."

"I do. It's in two days and I don't think I can get this place fixed up on time on my own. Can you come over and help me? I have snacks."

"I'll be right over as soon as I can."

"Great. Thanks!"

If Elizabeth was anything, she was punctual. She showed up at my house at half passed ten and we got straight to work. Thank god for her because I had somehow managed to waste away the morning hours trying to find what would look best where. Turned out my pile organizational system did no good at all. Before long we had started to make some real progress and my house was turning into a home.

"We've been at this for hours, want to break for a snack?"

"Beth, it's been forty five minutes."

"Are you kidding me?"

"No," she said, barely able to hold back her laughter. I felt a little hurt but brushed it off. I've been told many a time that I tend to be a little over sensitive. A quality I'm not proud of and one I wasn't ready to show to my new friend just yet. I kept my mouth shut and followed Elizabeth's instructions. We had found a system that worked for us, and within two hours - for real, we knew just about where everything would go. We placed the items in their proper rooms all in the center and covered with large plastic sheets I had ordered off Amazon. Some of the walls were painted a weird dirty yellow colour and I wanted to change that before I committed to hanging anything up or placing any furniture.

"Liz, wanna come with me to the hardware store real quick to get some paint?"

"I won't be able to come this time, I just got a text from the client I was with this morning apparently something is wrong with the backsplash tiles that were set to be put in later today. I gotta run. Talk later?"

"Sure thing."

I went to the hardware store by myself. The second I walked in I felt somewhat intimidated. Everyone in there looked like they were dressed for the part of hardware royalty and knew exactly what they were doing. I was sure I stood out like a sore thumb. I ducked my head down and tried to hide behind my hair. Now would have been a perfect time to test out whether or not I liked wearing baseball hats. Thanks to my attempt at disguising myself, I ended up walking right into a display of windshield wiper fluid and the bottles went rolling everywhere. I was mortified. I rushed as fast as I could to pick up every bottle in sight.

"Excuse me miss. I think you missed one." I turned around and thought I was dreaming. Was Jack Hunter really standing in front of me right now.

"I thought that was you Bethany. Oh my gosh get over here." Jack pulled me into a hug and it was as if I were transported right back into high school. I'll always remember the first time I laid eyes on Mr Jack Hunter all those years ago. I had never come across a boy with so many manners. It was my first day of high school and to say that I was nervous would be a large understatement. I thought I needed to look my very best which I now realize was silly.

I ended up being late for class and running through the halls of a building I was not familiar with. I wasn't looking and ran right into Jack, spilling my books and the entire contents of my back pack all over the halls - kind of like what I just did in the isle of the hardware store. Anyways, he told me I should be more careful and watch where I was going then walked off. I remember thinking he was so rude and just like all the other boys, but then he came back. He was holding my water bottle that had rolled so far down the hall I hadn't noticed it myself. He handed it to me, smiled and introduced himself, extending his hand to help me up off the ground. I already knew who he was but acted as if I didn't. I couldn't get over how polite he was. We became best friends. He was kind of like a brother to me - a protector. Although, everyone else around town seemed to think there was more to it.

"We've got to stop meeting like this Beth." I just smiled at him, remembering the day we officially met.
"Well at least I'm not late for class and my braces are gone."
"You'd still be Bethany to me."
"Oh stop it. How long has it been. You look exactly the same."

"Well going on twelve years I suppose. Since you left without a word after high school."

"Don't do that. You know I had to leave. I wanted more than what I could get from this town."

"Looks like you never found it since you're back now. Maybe what you needed was always right here and it took you leaving it all behind to realize it."

"Wow Jack, you've gotten deep over the years."

"What can I say. You learn a lot when you expected your life to go one way and out of nowhere it all changes. Searching for answers and finding oneself changes a man."

"What's that supposed to mean. What were you expecting?"

"I didn't mean anything by it."

"Liar."

"You've been gone for twelve years and the first thing you call me when you're back is a liar. Ouch."

"I can see you trying not to laugh, Jack."

"Alright you caught me. What are you doing in here anyways? I assume you didn't come all the way here to disturb the display?"

"Very funny. I'm here for paint samples for my house."

"You bought a house. You really are back for good then aren't you?"

"Here to stay."

"So what brings you back? How have you been?

I wanna hear it all Miss Bethany."
"Well the hardware store is hardly the place. Why don't you come over later and we can catch up for real."
"I'll see you later."

I watched him walk off down the isle, still in shock. Right from the start, he was always saving me from whatever messes I made. I had forgotten what his smile did to me. It was contagious. I could hardly wait to get home and tell Elizabeth about this one - she is going to get a kick out of this. I called her as soon as I got in.

"Guess what?"
"What?"
"You're supposed to guess."
"Uhm, you just won the lottery and now you're a millionaire?"
"Nice, but no. I just ran into Jack Hunter. Literally."
"Who's Jack Hunter?"
"Oh I'm surprised you haven't heard of him if I remember right I think he does construction around here."
"Name doesn't ring a bell, but if you seem this excited about it I'd love to meet him."
"He was my best friend in high school. I haven't seen him for years."

"Just your friend."

"Yes just my friend. Boys and girls can be friends contrary to popular opinions."

"I'm just messing with you."

"I know. Anyways, he's coming over later to catch up. You should swing by."

"Ah man I'd love to, but I'm still stuck with my client from earlier. I think it's going to be a long night."

"Really. That's too bad."

"Next time."

"Okay."

By the time I saw Jack pulling into my driveway, I had tried on at least twelve different outfits and half as many hair styles. I don't know why I was so anxious, it was just Jack. My friend Jack. He still dressed the same way he did in high school. Dark and mysterious from head to toe, but with the sweetest soul. His hair was shorter, but still long enough that he could run his fingers through those dark curls. He came inside and we got to talking. Conversation always came naturally between us. There was something about him that made me feel comfortable. And then he asked that dreaded question.

"So Beth, my parents heard about your husband."
"Oh."
"Aiden was his name?"
"Yeah."
"I wish I could have met him."
"I think you guys would have gotten along great," I
said through blurry eyes.
"Is that what brought you back to Corner Brook?"
"Yeah I guess so."
"Do you mind if I ask what happened?
I took a deep breath and recounted the day that
plays over and over in my mind for the very first
time out loud.
"Aiden was a longshoreman, but he worked part
time as a roadie for bands who needed the help.
He loved doing it so he didn't mind the long hours.
He was on tour working for the White Stripes. The
same tour that I coincidentally had tickets for. It was
a Friday night and school was out for the weekend.
I was headed up to Vancouver from Kelowna with
my roommate Sophia to see the show. We snuck
around the back of the building looking for the bus
and that's when Aiden found us. He was unloading
equipment and at first it was everything but love at
first sight. He was nice though and gave Sophia and
me backstage passes. We later bumped into him at
a bar in town and got to talking. We hit it off and
took it from there. We got married four years later.

I never imagined it would have ended the day that it did. It was a normal Tuesday for us. I was seeing one of clients who was due to give birth any day - if you didn't know I was a doula. Aiden kissed me goodbye and left for work. It had gotten pretty late and supper was getting cold. It wasn't like him to be late from work and not call to let me know, so I was beginning to worry. I called a few times but he wasn't picking up - that's when a few of his buddies from work came to the door. I had never seen them looking so serious, they were always all laughs and goofing around. When I opened the door, they started to cry. It was David, Aiden's best friend who had to tell me he passed away. He slipped and fell when he was unloading a shipment and didn't get back up. The guys thought he was pulling a prank to try freak them out but when he didn't respond they knew something more was going on. By the time he got to the hospital he was already gone. They said it was a ruptured brain aneurysm. Apparently people can live years with an aneurysm without even knowing it's there. They said the way that he fell is what caused it to rupture. He was only thirty two years old."

"Bethany I am so sorry. I can't even begin to imagine what you've been through."

"Thank you. That's the first time I said all of that out loud to anyone. It kind of felt good, like it was needed."
"Well I'm glad I was the one to listen. Is there anything I can do to help you get settled in?"
"No that's okay. Thanks again Jack."
"What for?"
"For being you. For listening."

6

I was almost as nervous for tonight as I was last night when I was waiting for Jack. The night of the first official meeting of our support group has finally rolled around. The feelings of excitement and nerves were very well balanced as I was thrilled to have my new friends over but very anxious about how the meeting will go. I think it definitely helped that I was able to tell Jack about Aiden. Saying the words out loud to another person warmed me up to being able to say it to three more tonight. My guests arrived one by one, Elizabeth was first because she offered to come before everyone else to help me with any setting up that needed to be done. Ethan and Gloria followed shortly after, completely disregarding the old saying of being fashionably late. We had planned for the meeting to start at seven and they walked in just after a quarter to, but I didn't mind. They remained standing awkwardly in the little entry way of my house until I escorted them to the living room. I was surprised at Gloria's behavior, I still didn't know her too well, but she seemed awfully tamed compared to her usual big personality. Ethan on the other hand had no trouble making himself right at home on my couch.

I couldn't help but smirk a little at the utter opposite
people than the ones I had grown used to. Before
long everyone warmed up to one another or so I
thought - until Ethan pulled me aside. He had been
eyeing me from across the room for five minutes.
At first I thought he had some kind of weird eye tick
but when he coughed and not at all subtly tilted his
head towards the kitchen I figured he wanted to talk.
"Um Ethan, do you think you could help me out in
the kitchen for a minute please?"
"I would be delighted my dear," he said in a mock-
ing way.
"What is your problem?"
"Well it took you long enough to realize I had one.
Did you not see me staring at you?"
"I thought you had some kind of eye thing."
"Eye thing? What? No. It's about your friend."
"Elizabeth? What about her?"
"That's just it, I don't know."
"You lost me."
"Something is off about that girl. I can't quite put
my finger on it but I will."
"Are you alright? You sound crazy."
"Rude but okay. I'm perfectly fine but your friend
is not." He said the word friend while making air
quotes with his fingers.
"Well I don't know what you want me to tell you.
There's nothing wrong with Elizabeth. You just met

 her. Try giving her a fair chance before you go all crazy on me."

"Whatever." He stormed back into the living room to join Elizabeth and Gloria who seemed to be hitting it off rather nicely.

"What was that all about?" Asked Gloria.

"Oh I just thought Ethan might like giving me a hand with the snacks - which I forgot in the kitchen. I'll be right back."

I stalled for a few moments more than necessary talking myself into going out there and telling them my story. I was able to tell Jack so why couldn't I tell them. "Alright, who wants a drink?"

"Me," said all three of them at the same time - it was actually kind of cute. I poured wine for everyone, downed mine in two sips and marched to the front of the living room so I was standing before everyone. They all looked at me, giving me their full attention probably wondering what on earth I was doing.

"Okay ladies and gentleman, I'm ready."

"Seriously," said Ethan.

"Seriously. So grab your drinks and sit tight before I lose my will to do this." All three of them looked at me then at each other wide eyed. They all knew how nervous and reserved I had been about opening up. I reached out my hand and Gloria gave me her

glass of wine. I finished hers too, with one big gulp
and began.

"His name was Aiden. I met him when I was twenty
four years old. He was twenty six. At first I wanted
nothing to do with him - I quickly found out that I
couldn't have been more wrong…" I went on to tell
them the whole story, the same I had told Jack, not
sparing them any details. When I was done I just
stood there. Had this been a normal meeting I would
have been able to get up and leave, running to the
comfort of my own home - but I already was home.
Gloria quickly caught on to what was happening
and came up to me and held my hands in hers. "I
knew you could do it," she said, giving me that
Gloria smile that I now felt comforted by in such
a short period of time. There was just something
about her that made me feel like everything would
be okay, that things always turned out the way they
were supposed to. I hoped some of her positivity
and healthy outlook on life would rub off on me.

"It was exactly one year ago yesterday." We all
turned to the couch where Elizabeth was sitting. It
took me a moment to understand what was happening. "Sometimes when I fall asleep I still forget,
then in the morning when I realize I'm sleeping
alone it all comes flooding back to me."

She was telling her story. She really listened to what I said and took the meeting seriously. I must admit I was so happy for her that she felt safe enough to open up to us, but I was also extremely intrigued to learn more about my best friend.

"We had been driving for hours. There was an amazing sale we couldn't pass up with so many good finds. I'm an interior designer and he is a contractor - was a contractor. We bought and sold houses that we flipped. We had started with nothing and built a pretty good living out of our little business. We were almost finished flipping the house we had been working on at the time, it was just missing a few small details. We had gone on these kinds of trips before but usually we took turns driving. Luke wasn't feeling well so I offered to drive the whole way home. He didn't like the idea but I insisted it was only fair because after all it was me who had pushed him to go on this particular trip. There was an antique lamp that I thought I needed. I told him it would tie together the entire house. I would trade that lamp in a heartbeat if it meant I could be with Luke again. We had been on the road since daylight and it was now dark. There weren't many street lights on that specific stretch of highway but I took it because it would get us home faster. It seems as though every decision I made that day was the wrong one. If I just would have listened to him he would still be here. Like I said, it was really dark and even my high beams weren't providing me with the kind of light I needed. I should have seen it coming but I didn't. There was construction work up ahead and the road was closed down to one lane. By the time I saw the trucks headlights they were blinding me which meant I was so close to the truck there was nothing else to do. I grabbed the wheel and swerved off the side of the road and the car just spun. It felt like it would never stop spinning. When we finally stopped rolling I grabbed my cell phone and clicked on the flashlight. I shook Luke and called his name over and over. No matter what I did he didn't respond. When the ambulance arrived they pulled us out of the car one by one and did all they could but his injuries were too severe. Everyone told me I was lucky to have survived but I felt everything but. I would have given anything to have been able to switch places with Luke. He should be here today. It was all my fault and now I have to live with it."

By this point she could barely talk let alone breath. She was sobbing so hard she jumped when I put my arms around her , she hadn't seen me get up from my seat and rush over to her. I now understood why she changed the subject so quickly the other night in the cafe. I felt kind of bad for being so intrigued by getting to hear her story. I saw a whole other side to my friend that night - one I wished didn't exist.

"Oh sweetheart come here," said Gloria. "None of that was your fault. You can't live your life thinking that it was. That's just no way to live."
"I know," she said through her sniffles. "It's just hard to accept that he's gone, even after all this time."

"I know. I sometimes forget myself that my husband is gone, but that might just be my age playing tricks on me." That line managed to shift the mood and get a smile out of Elizabeth. It was then that I realized how quiet Ethan was. He was sitting in the far corner of the room on a fold out chair I had brought in earlier. I looked him right in the eyes to try silently tell him he should get up and join us - say something to Elizabeth, at least try to get to know her, but he didn't budge. We all had a few more drinks and nibbled on some cheese and crackers. Before we knew it, the night had gotten away from us and everyone was getting ready to head out. We said our goodbyes but Gloria hung back from the others. She watched as both Ethan and Elizabeth got into their separate cars and drove away.

"Did you forget something Gloria?"
"Oh no."
"Okay. Did you want to come back in?"
"I just wanted to make sure you were alright before I left. I wanted to apologize for trying to convince you to get up the other night and tell your story. I had no idea."
"Oh that's okay, don't worry about it. I'll be alright."
"If you say so, but you know if you need me I'm a phone call away. I can be back here in ten."
"Thank you Gloria. Goodnight."

I had barely closed the door when my phone started to ring.
"Hello?"
"Hey, it's me," said Elizabeth.
"Oh hey, that was fast."
"I've been home for a few I was just giving Gloria a chance to leave. I noticed she was lingering. She seems very nice."
"Oh yeah she's great. So how do you think it went?"
"Not bad. You're right it was nice to open up."
"See I told you it would do you good."
"Oh fine you're Bethany knower of all things."
"Thank you. It's nice to hear it out loud from time

to time."

"Oh please. But for real, what's with the Ethan guy?"

"What about him?"

"He's kind of sketchy."

"How so?"

"Well for one, he kept staring at you like he has some kind of crush or something and —"

"Woah no slow your roll. He doesn't have a crush."

"I beg to differ. But let's say you're right, there's still something off about him. Why was he just sitting there in the corner. He didn't even say anything."

"Gloria didn't get up either."

"Okay. But you already know her story you told me about it remember?"

"Oh right."

"Have you ever even heard about why Ethan goes to support group?"

"No but —"

"Exactly."

7

I didn't sleep very well the night after the meeting at my house. It bothered me that Ethan didn't like Elizabeth. She had quickly become my best friend and I cared about her a lot. I may have been biased but no matter how hard I tried and believe me I did, I couldn't see what Ethan was seeing. There was nothing wrong with Elizabeth. Maybe she was right and he had feelings for me. That would make sense why he wanted to steer me away from her. I had been spending most of my free time with her. Speaking of, I decided to surprise her at her house with lattes and chocolate croissants from our cafe. I figured it was too early to go with the brownies we usually get. I was surprised to find she wasn't home. She hadn't told me that she would be out, but it was early and I suppose she didn't have to tell me everything she did. I really had to think about getting back to work. Not just for financial reasons, but I was afraid I might begin to slowly lose my mind without something to pass all the hours in the day. I just can't even think about going back to being a doula especially after Aiden and the baby. What was I to do now at my age, it was hardly the time to start a brand new career.

I called Liz and she picked up on the first ring.
"Hey Beth is everything alright? It's early."
"Oh yeah it's all good. I'm outside your house.
Where are you?"
"Oh crap didn't I tell you I usually go out for a run
in the mornings?"
"Nope. Must have slipped your mind. I can wait?"
"Sure thing, I'll be right there."

***

"Hey Beth. Sorry about that, I wasn't expecting
you."
"It's my fault. I should have called ahead. I brought
breakfast."
"Oh great thanks, I'm starved," she grabbed the bag
of croissants out of my hand, took a sip of her latte
and headed up the front steps to the door.
"Well, aren't you going to come in? You've waited
all this time."
"Oh yeah. Coming."

We walked into her house and I was just as mes-
merized as I had been the first time. I was a little
bit jealous of her knack for decorating but I would
never admit it out loud to her.

"I would offer you something, but it seems you've already got that covered."

"I don't like to show up places empty handed."

"That's something I can get used to. I'll have to invite you over more often," she said with a smile.

"Well now that you've let me in on your little plan you can think again lady."

"Darn you caught me."

"I have something to tell you."

"Ou what is it?"

"I have a date!"

"Oh lord please don't tell me it's with that Ethan guy. I might have to dis own you as a friend."

"Stop it. It's not with Ethan. It's with Jack."

"Ouu Jack. I can't wait to meet this mysterious Jack. You have to stop making all your plans with him on days that I'm busy. I need to make sure I approve of this man for my best friend."

"It's not like that. We're just hanging out. I've known him forever."

"Then why does your face look like that?"

"Like what?"

"All smiley and blushing."

"I am not!"

"You are though!"

"Whatever. Will you at least help me get ready without making fun of me. I'm nervous enough as it is."

"So you admit it, you liiiiike him."

"Fine I like him. It just feels weird. It's been a while since Aiden and I know he would want me to move on and be happy and I haven't felt the way I did around Jack since Aiden. I never meant for any of this we just started talking again the other day."

"But you never really forgot about Jack did you?"

"I guess not. I guess he's always been there in the back of my mind."

"Well then, let's get you dressed."

"I was just going to wear this," I said, motioning my arms down the length of my body.

"You know you're wearing old faded jeans and a t-shirt with a rip in the collar?"

"Yes. It's … edgy? Okay fine I help me."

By the time Elizabeth was done with me, I was in a floral print wrap dress that rested a few inches above my knees. It was a medium blue colour that I will admit was nice, with orchid coloured flowers scattered about the material. It had some small silver detailing that acted as leaves and vines connecting the flowers to one another. I drew the line when she tried to put me in a pair of heels. I don't do heels. I was lacing up my trusty pair of black converse in the kitchen when she came in holding something behind her back.

"Turn around."
"Show me what's behind your back first."
"Just trust me. It's nothing bad, promise."
"Fine."
"Lift up your hair please."

When I opened my eyes and looked down I saw that she had placed one of her necklaces on me. It was a small silver crescent moon. Very dainty and not something I would usually go for, but I liked it.

"This is beautiful, I couldn't possibly wear it."
"Oh please. If I didn't want you to wear it I wouldn't have offered."
"What if I lose it?"
"I'll have to kill you."
"What!"
"Geez. It's a joke. Please just wear it. It ties the whole look together. You'll be a complete mess without it."
"You're so dramatic. Fine I'll wear the necklace. Thank you."
"No thank you. By the way, I expect to hear all the juicy details the second you get home - that is unless you aren't alone," she said with a wink. "In that case, I can wait 'til morning for my info."
"You're ridiculous. I'll call you later."

Chelsea Robillard

8

I waited on the chair in my kitchen. For hours. I was afraid to move for fear of messing up my outfit. When boredom struck, I turned to my good old phone to keep me company. That's when I remembered I forgot it at Elizabeth's. It must still be in the pocket of my jeans that I had been wearing earlier. I swore if my head wasn't screwed on, I might forget that someplace too. At least I had my laptop. When I opened it I already had an email from Liz telling me about my phone. She said she would drop it off before she left to run errands but I told her not to bother - I could swing by after my date with Jack. Jack who was once again headed up my front walk way towards the door. He was early. I straightened out my dress and fluffed around with my hair before opening the door.

"Hey Beth, ready to go? You look beautiful."
"Thank you so do you. I mean handsome. You look handsome."
"Do I make you nervous," he asked with a hint of a smirk.
"Not at all," I replied as smoothly as I could while I bumped into the door frame and landed right in his

arms. "This is going well."

"C'mon let's go. We don't wanna miss the movie."
I should have known he would take me to a scary
movie, he did always have a thing for them. Some
people just liked the idea of getting scared, if I
remember correctly he used to say it was a good
adrenaline rush. Personally I think he's just nuts. I
couldn't tell you what the movie was about if you
asked me, I watched the majority of it through the
spaces between my fingers. My head was buried in
Jack's shoulder for the rest of it.

"Jack Hunter, did you just take me there so you
could get your arm around me?"
"I don't know what you mean?"
"Oh don't even try pull that one on me. I know you
remember how much those movies terrify me."
"They do?" He asked playfully as we walked hand
in hand down the main road. I lightly shoved him
in an attempt to flirt - something I was never really
good at.

"I have one more surprise for you miss Bethany."
"Oh lord. I don't know whether to be excited or
scared."
"Oh c'mon I'm not that bad. Am I?"
"No of course not, I'm just bugging you."
"Follow me."

I knew he wanted it to be a surprise. I could tell by the childish grin on his face, but it didn't take me long to know exactly where we were going. I didn't let him know that I knew anything, I was too happy watching him smile. He took me to the park where we spent most of our time in the summers and weekends throughout high school. Every good time, bad time was spent right here in this park. It's where I found Jack after his grandmother had passed away. It's where we came to celebrate when we passed all of our finals, and it's where I told Jack about my father, the day my parents told me that the man I always knew as dad was not actually my biological father. It was heavy for sure but in the end it didn't change anything, he was still dad to me.

"You can drop the act now. I know you knew where we were going."
"What ever do you mean?"
"Stop it. I would be offended if you didn't know. We basically grew up right here in the park. If you forgot it would feel as though you forgot about me."
"I would never."

It was in that moment that I saw Jack for the first time after all these years. I mean really saw him. I felt something inside of me shift. I know it sounds ridiculous but it was like straight out of one of those

movie scenes when the girl finally sees what's been right in front of her all along and the whole world stops spinning and just for a brief moment you're the only two beings on the planet. Then I was pulled right back down to earth when Jack said "I bet I can still beat you to the other end of the park."
"In your dreams, buddy."
We raced across the long stretch of grass and of course Jack won, I knew he would. I had tried so hard that I began to lose control of my legs and couldn't stop when I ran right into Jack who wasn't expecting it - we both went crashing into the grass laughing. I had landed right on top of him and he was looking at me in a way he never had before, or at least if he did I never noticed. It all happened so quickly but we kissed. I wanted to stay there in that moment just a little while longer and let the fireworks in my head finish their show, but I swore I saw a figure off in the distance watching us.
"Did you see that?"
"See what?"
"I swear there was someone down there a minute ago… watching us."
"Are you sure? I'll go take a look around. Stay here."
"No Jack, let's just get out of here."
"Alright, let's go."

He took me by the hand and we walked in step down the familiar roads we always used to as teenagers. "Oh my gosh no way. It's still there!"
"Just as you left it."
"Can we go? Please?"
"C'mon, I'm sure my parents would be thrilled to see you."

You know how close I was with Jack, well I was just as close with his parents. It was like my very own second set of parents. Don't get me wrong I love my mom and dad more than words can say, but if there was ever something I wasn't ready to go to them with, I knew I could always come here. I spent many hours here, rocking on the antique white porch swing. I always loved it. I thought it was so beautiful and elegant. It made me feel like a flower princess when I swung on it. I couldn't believe that after all these years it was still here. I swung and caught up with Jack's mom as he and his dad chatted inside. We only left because we realized how much time had gotten away from us and it was actually really late. We walked back to the theatre where Jack's car was parked waiting for us and he drove me home. I didn't want the night to end but I knew it wouldn't be a good idea for me to invite Jack inside and I knew he wouldn't ask if not offered. He kissed me goodnight on the cheek and walked me to my door. What a gentleman. I watched as he got back into his car and began to drive away. Before he was completely out of sight, I was already dialing Elizabeth's cell. She didn't listen after all and had dropped my stuff off in my mailbox. Thank god because I got so caught up on my date I never made it around to her place to pick up my things. She picked up on the first ring.

"How was it?"
"It was so good."
"Did you guys kiss?"
"We did," I squealed like a little school girl, surprising myself. I didn't know I had that in me.
"Omg I knew it."
"Yeah yeah we're adorable."
"Did he like the outfit?"
"He did actually he told me I looked nice."
"What about the necklace?"
"Yes he liked that too."
"Ha. I told you it finished the look."
"I know I know you were right. But something weird happened."
"Oh no was the kiss bad?"
"No nothing about Jack. We went to the movies and it was the strangest thing, I could have swore I saw Ethan in the same theatre as us. I got up to check but there was no one in the lobby."

"That is weird. I told you something was off about that guy. Don't hang around with him if you're on your own. Did you tell Jack?"

"No. I didn't want to worry him, but then we were in the park goofing around and I thought I saw someone off in the distance watching us."

"Are you serious? Did you call the police?"

"No. Jack wanted to go check things out, but I just wanted to leave so I convinced him not to go look."

"That's crazy. At least you had Jack with you. And thank goodness you're both okay."

"I know."

"Did you want me to come over for a bit so you aren't alone?"

"No, thanks anyways but it's not necessary I'll be alright."

"Okay if you're sure. If you change your mind give me a call. No matter what time."

"Thanks Elizabeth."

"No worries. I know you would do the same."

9

The next morning I had plans to meet Elizabeth at the cafe for lunch. It was a nice change since we had only been the one other time during the day. It was a complete different atmosphere seeing things through the light of the sun. This time I got there first, but I wasn't worried about keeping up appearances like I had been last time. I felt our friendship was growing strong and I could be myself without worrying about how it looked if I showed up a little early. I liked being early, so showing up fashionably late was actually much harder for me. I just had time to put in our orders as Elizabeth came rushing into the cafe.

"Sorry I'm late I lost track of time."

"That's not like you. I'll let it slide this one time."

"Oh gee thanks so much."

"I got our usual."

"Oh you didn't have to do that, thanks Beth. I'll transfer you the money later."

"Don't even think about it, this ones on me."

"Thanks girl. Oh hey look who it is. Gloria, hi, over here."

"Well hello girls, this is a nice surprise."

"For us too," I added. I made a mental note to invite Gloria along next time we had one of these girl dates. I don't know why I didn't think of it before. "May I?"

"Oh please, of course join us, can I get you anything?"

"Thanks Beth but I've already put in my order. What brings you ladies to the cafe. I don't believe I've seen you guys here before. Have you tried the green juice? It's to die for," said Gloria as she placed her palm over her forehead and tipped her head back mocking a woman in distress.

"Actually," I said, "This is where we officially met."

"You wouldn't say."

"Yeah it was right after she met you at the meeting," added Elizabeth.

"Well two gems in one night. That was quite the find you had Bethany."

None of us could hold it in, we all busted out laughing with that one. We chatted for a while and both Liz and myself kindly declined when Gloria asked us if we wanted to share her green juice.

"Gloria, if you don't mind, there was something I wanted to ask you about Ethan."

"Alright, what is it?"

"Well at first I didn't think anything of it, but Elizabeth here got the feeling something was off about him the other night at my house.

I told her she was mistaken, but I had a date last night," she smiled at me discreetly when I added that in, " and I swore I saw Ethan in the same movie I was in. Then later on I'm almost positive we were being watched in the park."
"And you think it was Ethan?"
"Well that's just it, I don't know. I wanted to get your input on the whole thing before I said anything to him."
"I wouldn't worry dear. Ethan appears to be confidant and outgoing maybe even a little arrogant at first glance, but underneath it all he's actually quite shy and reserved since his partner passed away."
"Oh. I didn't mean anything by it, I hope you know. I was just wondering."
"When the time is right I'm sure he'll tell you all he wants you to know."
"One more thing?"
"Shoot."
"Elizabeth thinks Ethan has a crush on me."
"I wouldn't worry about that dear," she said as she walked off giggling and mumbling to herself. "See you tomorrow night ladies."

"That was weird," said Liz.
"What?"

"She totally brushed off what you were trying to tell her about Ethan."

"I don't think that's how it was at all. She knows him much better than either one of us do. Maybe this whole thing is one big misunderstanding."

"Maybe. But I still don't trust him as far as I can throw him."

"Well then I guess you don't trust him at all by the looks of those arms."

"Shut up. Hey was that your phone?"

"Oh yeah it was. Hold on a sec."

"Who is it?"

"It's Sophia. My roommate from college. She's coming to visit in a few days. You kind of remind me of her."

"Do I get to meet her?"

"Of course, if you want?"

"Awesome, let's get to planning some fun things we can all do together."

10

The following morning I found myself back at the
cafe. I had been spending more time there than
at my actual house. After I left the cafe yesterday
afternoon, I said goodbye to Elizabeth and went
to meet up with Jack. My whole mood changed
when I was around him. He really brought out the
best in me. Sometimes I forgot that I had left for so
long, but I can't say I regret doing so. I will always
cherish my time with Aiden. I haven't seen him for
a while now, I suppose he knows I'm doing okay
so he doesn't feel as though he has to stop by and
check on me as often.

I had gotten a table for three this morning as I
waited for my friends to show up. Ethan got here
first and I couldn't help but feel a little uneasy that I
would be alone with him until Gloria got here. I did
feel bad about it though, I didn't want to feel that
way around him. I guess the recent events have just
gotten into my head a little.
"Good morning stranger."
"Hey Ethan. Where's Gloria?"

"Who knows with that one. I'm sure she's on her way. Mind if I have a seat?"

"No go for it, that's what they're here for." I could feel the awkward vibes practically spilling off of me and I assumed that my face wasn't helping in hiding how I felt - I never was good at hiding my emotions.

"Is everything alright Beth?"

"Yeah why?"

"Well usually if you had something to tell us, you would just say it online in the group chat. What's so important that you had to have us meet you here?"

"Let's just wait until Gloria gets here."

"Alright. In the mean time, why don't we get better acquainted. After all I don't really know much about you, nor you about me."

"That's true, you first. What do you do for a living?"

"I'm retired now but I was a police officer."

"No way."

"What's that supposed to mean?"

"Nothing I'm sorry. I just never would have guessed."

"That's quite alright, I get that more than you might think."

"You seem pretty young to be retired. What's the story there if you don't mind me asking?"

"Maybe we better save that for — oh look at that saved by the bell, here comes Gloria. Over here sugar."

"Good morning my little friends."

"Hey there Gloria, thanks for meeting me here."

"What is it that's so important you have me here at the crack of dawn?"

"Gloria, it's almost ten in the morning," I said with a laugh.

"Oh never mind."

"So," said Ethan, questioningly.

"Alright alright. So Gloria as you know I've been spending a lot of time with Jack lately. He was actually the first person I told about Aiden. I mentioned our group to him and he thinks it's really nice that we've created a safe place where we can open up and help each other. I was wondering if it would be alright with you guys if I invited him to come along tonight?"

"Of course," said Gloria. "I would love to meet this Jack I've been hearing about."

"Is he in the same situation as us," asked Ethan.

"Well not really. He hasn't lost anyone in the way that we have, he would be there more for support."

"I thought this was supposed to be a safe place where we could feel comfortable to open up and you want to bring in a stranger?"

"I'm sorry Ethan I didn't think it would upset you this much." I was beginning to wonder if maybe Elizabeth was right after all and maybe Ethan really did have feelings for me. He didn't get so offended when I suggested inviting Liz into the group.
"No it's fine. Invite him."
"Okay. I'll see you guys later I guess."

I walked out of the cafe before Ethan changed his mind or I got the courage to give him a piece of mine. Before I was out of earshot I saw Gloria lean over the table and whisper something to Ethan. I didn't catch it all but I know for a fact I heard her say "You'd better tell her soon. She's starting to question things." I had no idea what that was meant to imply and as a matter of fact I wasn't so sure I even wanted to know. I erased the memory from my mind for the time being and dialed Jack's number as I walked home.

"Good morning Beth."
"Good morning Jack."
"What's up?"
"I have something to ask you."
"What is it?"
"Are you free tonight?"
"Maybe, what did you have in mind?"

"Remember that support group I was telling you about? The one I started with my friends that I hold at my house?"

"Yes, but what does that have to do with us — oh no Beth I can't come to that?"

"Why not?" I asked. Feeling slightly offended.

"Don't get mad, it's not like that at all. I just don't want to crash something that I have no business being at."

"I already checked with everyone and they didn't mind."

"Alright I'll be there."

"Awesome. See you later. It starts at seven."

I hung up the phone just as I was approaching my front door. I felt as though my impeccable timing was a sign from above that today was going to be a good day. I hadn't told Elizabeth about Jack coming to the meeting. I knew I didn't have to check with her first since she had been dying to meet him. I called her right away to surprise her with the good news.

"Liz guess what!?"

"If you're on your way over here, turn around."

"What? No. I have a surprise for you."

"Is it a bucket of chicken noodle soup?"

"What are you talking abo—" I was interrupted by a giant sneeze followed by a fit of coughing. "Liz are you alright?"

"Oh just dandy. I have the flu."

"No. No. No. You can't be sick."

"Why not?"

"We have support group tonight at my house and I invited Jack. That was the surprise. You were finally going to get to meet him."

"Oh Beth I'm so sorry. I can try to make it there."

"No that's alright. You have to rest, and you don't want to give all of us the flu too."

***

"Ethan, Gloria, this is Jack. Jack, Ethan and Gloria."

"Hello everyone, it's nice to meet you and put some faces to the names. Beth here has told me so much about you, all good."

"Likewise," said Gloria.

"Where's Elizabeth," asked Ethan. "I have trouble believing she would miss this."

"She's sick."

"How convenient," he said.

"I don't know what that's supposed to mean but I spoke to her on the phone earlier and she sounded awful."

"Forget her then. So Jack, what brings you to the

meeting?"

"Actually Bethany invited me. I said no at first,
I didn't want to put my nose where it doesn't belong."

"So you haven't lost anyone?"

"Not in the way you all have. My condolences by
the way. The closest I've ever come to losing someone was when I split with my ex girlfriend. Things
got pretty ugly in the end."

"How so," asked Gloria as she poured herself a
glass of wine and scooted her chair closer to Jack. I
was glad she had already gotten so comfortable.

"Oh it's nothing crazy. A few years back I met this
girl online. I don't care much for the internet, but I
thought I would give it a try. We seemed to have a
lot in common. It went well for a while until things
started to get weird. She started calling me late at
night and leaving me creepy love notes around my
construction sites. I'm a contractor here in town.
We had only been on a couple dates, so I thought it
was funny at first like she was trying to pull a prank
on me, but then she told me she was falling in love
with me. It came completely out of left field and
I didn't feel the same way at all. I crushed it then
and there and she seemed to be okay with it. Then I
noticed she started following me home from work
and she would just appear places that I was out of
nowhere. That was when I called it quits and had to

file for a restraining order."
Both Ethan and Gloria had gotten so close to Jack
in the midst of the story he had to take a few steps
back.

"That sounds like something out of a movie," said
Gloria.
"For real," added Ethan. "That really happened to
you?"
"I wish I could say it wasn't true, but yes."
I hadn't even heard the story in full and was just
as shocked as my friends. What if that's who was
watching us the other night in the park. I had almost
convinced myself that it was Ethan, but the figure
was so far away. It could have been a woman. I
couldn't help but let the thought cross my mind. I
shook it off along with the shivers that were creep-
ing up my spine.
"Are you alright Beth? You look like you've seen a
ghost."
"I'm fine Jack."
"What's her name?" Asked Ethan. "The crazy lady."
"Maia."

11

"Why didn't you tell me the whole story?" I asked Jack as I closed the door and waved goodbye to my guests.

"Because I knew you would be freaked out. I didn't want to worry you for no reason."

"No reason!?"

"She's no longer in my life. I haven't seen her in ages. I don't even think she still lives here in Corner Brook."

"How can you be sure?"

"Well I can't but according to her Facebook page she moved to Alberta months ago."

"Oh."

"Oh?"

"Oh as in oh I hadn't realized you had any proof. I thought you were just trying to make me feel better. I'm sorry."

"Don't be sorry. Come here," he said as he wrapped me up in one of his famous bear hugs. I just stayed there for a while, my head pressed up against his chest, letting all my worries wash away.

When I calmed down it dawned on me that Jack still hadn't met Elizabeth and I had the perfect idea to get them to become friends.

"Hey Jack. I have an idea."
"Oh boy what is it?"
"No really. It's a good one. My friend Elizabeth is an interior designer. She used to flip houses with her husband but he passed away."
"Oh man that sucks. What's with all these young healthy people leaving us way too soon."
"I know it's unfair. But, I was thinking, Elizabeth would be perfect if you ever thought you needed someone to help out with decorating. You always say it's not one of your strengths."
"I don't know Beth, it's always just been me and my team. I'm not sure I want to stir things up right now."
"She's really good at what she does."
"Okay, tell you what, I'll meet her and chat and take it from there. Sound good?"
"Perfect! Here's her number."
"Okay. I'll call her later."
"Oh no you won't. You'll call her right now while I'm here and I can be sure you're actually doing it."
"You always have been a little bossy haven't you."
"I would argue, but you're probably right."

"Here we go. Are you watching? I'm dialing…
Hello? Elizabeth?"
"Hi, this is Elizabeth. May I ask who I'm speaking
to?"
"This is Jack, Bethany's uh - friend."
"Oh my gosh, Jack! How nice to finally meet you,
well hear from you. It seems I'm always just missing you."
"So I've been told. Anyways. I don't know if Bethany mentioned it to you but I'm a contractor here
in town and may be in the market for someone who
knows a thing or two about decorating. I hear you
may be the lady for the job."
"You've heard right. This is such great news. Would
you like to set up a time to meet and further talk it
out?"
"How about that cafe you guys always go to?"
"Perfect. I'm busy the next two days. The one after
that?"
"See you there at noon."
"Bye Jack."

"Happy Beth?"
"Yes! Can I come with?"
"No."
"Fair enough."
"What do you have planned for the rest of the day?
Wanna go grab a bite?"

"Oh no. Is that really the time?"
"Yes. Why? Have some place you need to be?"
"Actually I do. I'm supposed to be at the airport really soon to pick up Sophia."
"Sophia, your college roommate, Sophia?"
"The one and only. I'll see you later?"
"Of course. Drive safe."

***

"Ahhh omg it's really you!"
Sophia dropped her bags right where she was standing and abandoned them in the middle of the airport to run over to me. She jumped right into my arms, but I would have expected nothing less from her.

"I can't believe you're actually here in Corner Brook. How was your flight?"
"Boring. All the movies sucked." Typical Sophia I thought to myself as I laughed it off and reminded her that all of her things were still unguarded where she had dumped them moments before.

"Oh crap," she said as she pushed her way passed a large crowd moving quickly in the opposite direction. The drive back to my place was anything but quiet. I barely managed to get a word in with all of the stories Sophia had to tell about all of her yoga adventures. I liked to listen to them and imagine myself there because I knew it wasn't the lifestyle for me so living it through Sophia worked out perfectly.

"This is your house?"
"It is. You like?"
"I love! It's so … you!"
"Is that supposed to be an insult?"
"Not at all. Who do you think I am. If I was insulting you, you would know cause I would tell it to you straight."
"Very true."
"I love what you've done with all of the decor. Everything really goes together so well."
"I can't take all the credit for that I had a lot of help."
"Oh?"
"Yeah from Elizabeth. The girl I was telling you about. We've been spending a lot of time together and she's actually an interior designer so she offered to help me get the place fixed up to my liking."
"How generous of her. I'll have to meet this Elizabeth."
"Am I sensing a hint of jealousy there?"
"Me, no never."

We both laughed at Sophia's delivery, but I could see it in her eyes that she was a little hurt at how close I had gotten with Elizabeth in such a short amount of time.

"Well I'm beat," said Sophia.

"Follow me your royal highness. Let me show you up to your humble abode."

"It's about time someone recognizes me for who I am."

The two of us cracked up laughing as I showed Sophia to the guest bedroom. She was out like a light before I had the time to get her blanket and pillows on the bed.

12

We spent the following morning cooped up in the house because Sophia insisted I tell her absolutely everything that has happened from the moment I got here "not leaving anything out," to quote her. If you thought I could be persuasive, you should meet Sophia. I recounted my short time back in Corner Brook, starting with Elizabeth.

"I guess I'll start with Liz since she was the first person I met, technically."
"Ou Liz. You even have cute little nicknames."
"I thought you said you weren't jealous?"
"I thought you were going to tell me a story?"
"I would if you would let me."
"My bad," she said and went on to mock me in an attempt to annoy me.
"Okay so I was waiting for my luggage at the station when I saw this girl walking away with it."
"Let me guess, Elizabeth?"
"Yes. Shhh. I ran after her, got my stuff back blah blah blah. It wasn't until after my first attempt at support group that I saw her again in the cafe I ran in to get out of the rain. It was all sheer coincidence which worked out in my favor. We really hit it off

- but I should admit I went to the lengths to make sure we did."

"What exactly is that supposed to mean, Beth? Did you do something crazy?"

"No. I mean I don't think so. I was really lonely and desperate for a friend so I cyber stalked her. Turns out we have a lot of things in common so it wasn't that hard to get her to like me. I had to make the first move but then things just happened rather naturally."

"It kind of sounds like you were trying to date this girl."

"Gosh no. I told you I was desperate okay. You were off doing whatever you do and Aiden was well, I was all alone."

"I'm so sorry, come here. I didn't mean to upset you. I know how much you've been going through. Have you decided when you're going to go back to work?"

"No. I don't see how I ever can. Not as a doula anyways."

"Because of the baby?"

"Yes. Please don't say anything around anyone. You're still the only one that knows. I didn't even tell my parents - it would crush them."

"My lips are sealed. But do you think maybe you should talk to someone about it, like professional-ly?"

"And say what? That I can't go back to work as a doula because the stress of my thirty two year old husband dropping dead one day caused me to lose my baby? What good will that do. Unless I'm meeting with some sort of wizard who can turn back time, I'm out of luck."

"Alright, I get it. Tell me more about these Ethan and Gloria people I've heard you mention."

"There's not much to tell. I met them in support group. It was Gloria who decided we should start a group of our own to help me open up. She's very intuitive, she could sense that I was having trouble with the idea of speaking in front of all those people at the meeting. She's a real free spirit if I've ever met one. She taught art at the local high school, she's retired now. She believes that art is therapy and took her job very seriously. She's been trying to get me to sign up for a painting class with her, she says it would do me some good. Who knows, maybe I'll take her up on the offer."

"Maybe you should, and while I'm here so I can tag along."

"We'll see."

"Hmm Okay. And this Ethan guy, any sparks there?"

"First of all, no and second, did you hear nothing when I told you about Jack?"

"Right."

"I don't really know much about Ethan. He seems nice, very loud and confident personality but when it comes to his personal life he shies away and gets very reserved. I haven't been able to figure him out. He pulled me aside the other night and told me that he thought something was off about Elizabeth and she said the same about him. I don't know who to believe. Liz thinks he likes me and doesn't like her because we spend so much time together. But there was one weird thing that I never really figured out fully. Remember when I told you I was going on a date with Jack?"

"Yeah. You guys went to the movies. Ha - see I do listen."

"Anyways, I swore I saw Ethan walk into the same showing we were in. When I went to took for him he was gone. But later that night we were at the park and I saw someone - a figure off in the distance and wondered if maybe it could have been him."

"Why are you only telling me all of this now!?"

"There was no reason to freak you out. You couldn't have done anything from the other side of the country."

"I could have told you to call the police, which I assume you did."

"That's exactly what Elizabeth said, but I didn't actually."

"What! Why not?"

"Ethan is the police - or he was."

"Woah. I swear I've been listening to every word, but you just lost me there."

"I just found out the other day. It's like the only thing I know about him. He's retired now, I don't know the whole story, or any of it for that matter but he used to be a police officer."

"Did you ask Gloria?"

"I did. She said he would tell me what he wanted me to know when the time was right."

"Weird."

"Yeah. And the other day when I was leaving the cafe, I over heard Gloria whisper to Ethan that 'he should tell me soon.'"

"Omg tell you what?"

"I don't know. I didn't ask."

"What is wrong with you woman? Do I have to do all the super sleuthing around here? Where does this Ethan guy live?"

"I don't even know his last name but you think I know where he lives? You're funny."

There was a silence for a brief moment as I could see the wheels in Sophia's mind turning. "Hold that thought would ya," I said as the doorbell rang saving me from whatever form of interrogation was about to ensue.

I opened the door, only half of my attention focused on whoever was awaiting and the other half on Sophia as she rambled on about something. When I looked up I practically chocked on my words when I saw Ethan standing on my door step with donuts and coffee in his hands and a forced smile on his face.

"Can I come in?"

13

"Sure. What are you doing here Ethan? Did we have plans I forgot about?" I knew full well we did not have any plans but I was trying to play it cool and hide my concern. I looked over at Sophia who was also trying to keep her cool. How long had he been standing out there? Could he have heard us talking about him?

"No not that I know of. I just figured it was about time I shared a little bit about myself with you."
"And that's my cue to get on out of here to give you too some privacy," said Sophia.
"You don't have to do that, Soph. I'm sure Ethan doesn't mind. Right?"
"It's all good. I want to explore where you grew up anyways. Text me when you're done and you can come meet me wherever I end up."
I gave her a look that I knew she would understand. A look that said what do you think you're doing, don't you dare leave me alone with him, but she left anyways.
"So, Ethan."

"I'm gonna stop you right there Bethany. I know this may seem weird, but I've heard that you were asking around about me."

"Let me guess, Gloria?"

"I'm not even going to try to deny it."

"I should have known she couldn't keep a secret. She likes to meddle doesn't she?"

"You don't even know the half of it."

"Would you like to sit down?" I had been so taken aback by Ethan's surprise visit that I lost all sense of manners. We had been awkwardly standing in the entry way for far too long.

"I would love to, thanks. I'm going to get right to it and be straight with you."

"I would appreciate that."

"Alright, where do I start. Let's see, you know I used to be a police officer so we can scratch that off the list."

"Why don't you start with what lead you to attend support group?" I could sense his nerves so I felt I needed to chime in to break the ice a little and help get the ball rolling.

"Right. It's been about five years now. Since the accident and the day I left the police force. My partner's name was Dylan, we met when I was sill in school. He would come in from time to time to help out with certain courses. He didn't seem like the kind of guy I would normally get along with, our personalities couldn't have been more opposite, but that quickly changed when we were paired together. He had recently lost his partner and was in the market for a new one. The decision really wasn't up to me at all, so I had no say in the matter. I was hesitant at first and feared that he would be hard on me, but we actually got along quite well. I had been working with him my entire career as a police officer, he taught me everything I knew. That's why when I heard what had happened, I almost didn't believe it until I rushed over to the scene and saw it with my own eyes. If there was one thing that he taught me that would always stick, it was never go in alone, no matter the situation. Always wait for backup - but for some reason he didn't. That day I saw first hand why he drilled that statement into my head time and time again. We had worked a full shift and I was headed home - I thought Dylan was too, but he heard a call come in through his radio and was only two blocks away. It was a shooting that involved children, part of me understands why he did what he did. He called for backup, I heard it on my radio - we always liked to keep them turned on even when we were off duty for instances like this one. I guess he figured he could handle it on his own until back up arrived, but the situation had escalated more than he had anticipated and by the time I got to the scene, well, he was gone."

"Oh Ethan, I'm so sorry. I never should have questioned you, I didn't know."

"It's alright, I understand. I judged you at first as well. As for Elizabeth's theory that I have a crush on you —"

"Gloria didn't hold anything back did she."

"She didn't, but I can assure you that she was right when she said not to worry about it. Dylan wasn't just my partner on the job, he was my partner in life."

When he said those words, I remember just being at a standstill as if someone had pressed the pause button on me and I couldn't move. I felt so horrible for Ethan - both for what he had gone through and for the way I had turned on him so quickly without allowing him the chance to tell me his side of things.

"I don't even know what to say Ethan."

"You don't have to say anything, I know you understand what it feels like to lose someone you love. I'm just happy you and Jack found each other."

"Thank you — Oh would you excuse me for a second that's my phone. I better check in case it's Sophia, she could have gotten herself lost."

"Go for it. She seems like a nice girl by the way."

"Yeah she's pretty great. Seems she found the famous cafe, here look at this selfie she sent of her with a latte."

"Well I don't want to keep you. I've said my piece

so I should be on my way."

"Are you sure? You're more than welcome to come with me to the cafe to meet Sophia."

"Thanks for the offer, but I think I'm going to pass on this one. I'll see you around."

"Alright. Hey Ethan?"

"Yeah?"

"Thank you."

"For what?"

"For trusting me."

He smiled at me and for the first time I saw him for who he is. He has such kind eyes, I don't know how I missed that detail before.

I walked him out and then went in the opposite direction headed for the cafe. I was happy Sophia was seeing all of the things that I loved about my fresh start here in Corner Brook - I just wished we were doing it together. I hurried so I could get there before she finished her latte so I could get one of my own. I busted through the front door, waving at the baristas whom I had come to know rather well in such a short period of time. I looked all around, but the cafe was fairly small and I knew right away that Sophia was not in here.

14

"Excuse me. Hello! Has anyone seen this girl?" I made my way frantically through the maze of the cafe layout asking everyone in sight if they had seen Sophia. I pulled up the selfie she had sent me earlier and zoomed in on her face. I wasn't sure why I went directly into panic mode, I suppose you could say I just had a feeling something was wrong. I bumped into a woman and quickly apologized as I helped her pick up her belongings.
"My bad , I didn't mean to — Gloria?"
"Oh hi Beth, was that you running all around this place like a crazy person? I didn't have my glasses on."
"Yes. My friend is missing she was just here. She sent me this photo of her sitting right here in this cafe just a short while ago."
"Dear, calm down, take a breath. I'm sure she's fine and there's a reasonable explanation."
"I know. You're probably right. I'm panicking for no reason I guess I'm just a little on edge still after hearing about everything with Maia. I haven't been sleeping much."
"Let me see that picture of your friend again."

"Here."

"Well I've been in here for the past half hour and I haven't seen her, but then again you can't always rely on these old blinkers of mine. Why don't we go walk around outside a little. Some fresh air would do you good, and I'm sure we'll find your friend on the way."

"Sophia. Her name is Sophia."

"Well I'm sure we'll find Sophia."

Gloria and I spent the next little while walking around the surrounding streets of the cafe. I felt as though I had floated out of my body and I was watching us walk around from up above - it was the strangest feeling. No matter what Gloria said to reassure me, I could not calm down. Why would she tell me she was at the cafe and then not be there when I showed up?

"So, Beth. Am I any closer to getting you to agree to come to an art class with me?"

"Oh, I don't know Gloria. It's not really my thing."

"What are you talking about! Art is everyones thing. You just have to feel it out and let the art come from within."

"You know, sometimes you sound crazy."

"I've been told worse."

We both laughed at that, and in that moment I was thankful for Gloria. I embraced all of her crazy habits and free spirited ways. Without even trying, she had managed to bring me back down into my body and be present. There was a calming quality to her, almost motherly.

"So," said Gloria, "I heard you spoke with Ethan this morning."

"I did. Not nice lady, you could have told me he was gay when I was worried he had a crush on me."

"It was more fun for me to let it unfold on it's own."

"So you liked watching me squirm?"

"You were hardly squirming and besides I told you you had nothing to worry about."

"Well you could have gotten a little deeper in your confession don't you think?"

"I suppose."

"You know, I did mention the whole art class thing to Sophia, and she wants us to do it while she's in town so she can tag along."

"That would be great. As I always say, the more the merrier - for most things anyways."

"I don't even wanna know what you're referring to."

"Just use your imagination, you'll get there. Hey look, on your doorstep, is that your friend?"

"Omg Sophia! I'm going to kill you."

"Woah, rude much. What did I do?"

"Where were you?"

"Um here."

"Why did you tell me to come meet you at the cafe?"

"I didn't."

"You did. You sent that picture and I showed up and you weren't there."

"Yeah I sent the picture but I didn't tell you to come meet me."

"Yes you did, look — oh oops." I pulled up the message she had sent and saw that she was right. She was showing me that she had found the cafe I always tell her about, she never actually said to meet her there.

"I'm waiting," she said.

"For what?"

"My apology."

"In your dreams."

"Well what do you know, it was all just a misunder-standing," said Gloria. "I'm Gloria by the way, nice to meet ya."

"Oh yeah, Sophia, Gloria, Gloria, Sophia."

"Nice to meet you Gloria, I like your style! Very boho chic."

"Thank you dear, I'm glad somebody around here knows good style when they see it."

"I don't know if that's a personal dig at me, but I

don't care, I like the way I dress," I added.

"Yes. Very rocker, glam," said Sophia and her and Gloria laughed so hard I was surprised they didn't alert the neighbors.

"Say what you want, you're both jealous."

15

"That Gloria lady seems awesome," said Sophia. "I hope I'm like her when I'm that age."

"Yeah, she's pretty great."

"Oh Beth, I almost forgot. I have some crazy news to tell you."

"What?" After what Jack had told me about Maia and Ethan dropping that giant truth bomb on me earlier I wasn't sure I could handle anymore crazy in my life for a while.

"Do you remember the roommate I told you about? The one I was roomed with the semester you decided to live off campus to help out your parents?"

"Yeah what about her?"

"Well we didn't really know each other so well back then so I never told you the whole story about why I was so happy for you to come back to campus."

"I thought you were just excited because you missed me?"

"Now is hardly the time for that, obviously I missed you. Just listen I saw her today when I was at the cafe. I don't think she saw me though, that's why I left so quickly."

"And what's the big deal? You told me she was stealing things and didn't pick up after herself. So you hid from her?"

"That's just what I told you as a cover story. I had to give you some reason why I wanted you to move back in earlier than you were supposed to."

"So what did she do that was so bad you had to hide from her today? Did you even know she lived here?"

"No. I'm pretty sure I would have said something to you if I did, like warned you maybe or described her to you so you would know who to look out for."

"Why are you freaked out?"

"Because she scares me."

"How?"

"Everything was going great at first, until I made the mistake of telling her that you would be moving back in at the end of the semester. Apparently the housing department hadn't told her and she thought that she would be permanently roomed with me. From that moment on she got all weird and really shady. She was jealous every time I would bring up your name, that's why I never wanted her to meet you. She hated that fact that I had other friends than her. Do you remember that weekend I came up and stayed with you at your parents house?"

"Yeah."

"I told you I wanted to have a girls night, but really I needed to get away from her. From Hannah. She had completely lost her mind and found some of your clothes you left behind, she put them on and did her hair like yours - she literally dyed her hair to make it look like you. She was pretending to be you. She told me that she was so happy we were best friends and that we were going to live together."

"What?!"

"She was delusional. She was trying to replace you."

"Why am I only hearing this for the first time right now?"

"There was no point in telling you back then. I reported her to the school, they looked into it but found nothing. When I went back to the room on the Monday after I left your parents house, she was gone. Her side of the room was emptied out and just the way you had left it - it was as if she was never there. I tried to find her on social media but she had blocked me on everything and you were all set to move back in the following week. I laid low for a while and just waited things out. I never saw or heard from her again until today in the cafe."

"What is going on in this town?"

"I have no idea."

"Let's FaceTime Elizabeth to see if she knows any-

one named Hannah? She's been here longer than me, so maybe she's heard something."
"Yeah sure."

I Facetimed Elizabeth and she picked up on the second ring.
"Hey Beth, what's up?"
"Hey, I'm here with Sophia."
"Hi Elizabeth," Sophia yelled from across the room.
"I won't keep you you seem busy. I just have a quick question."
"It's fine, I'm just loading up the car I just finished grocery shopping."
"Nice sunglasses by the way are they new?"
"Yeah, Beth what was your question?"
"Oh right. Do you know anyone named Hannah?"
"Not that I can think of why? Should I?"
"Oh no, she's just someone Sophia knows and thought she saw today in the cafe. I just thought maybe you had heard of her."
"No sorry I'm afraid not, but if I hear anything I'll let you know. I'll search through my Facebook friends later, I accept almost anyone on there, who knows maybe we're friends and I didn't even know it."
"Thanks Liz, you're the best."
"Talk to you later. Nice meeting you Sophia."

"Back at ya," she yelled from the bathroom. "We'll have to hang out for real before I go back home."

"I don't want to just sit here and think about this right now, can we invite Jack over? I wanna meet this man who's got my best friend all giddy and what not."
"I am not giddy. Okay maybe I am just a little."

Jack was over within the next twenty minutes and Sophia wasted no time. She began her interrogation before the door had even closed behind him. He looked over at me periodically with a look that was begging to be saved, but I was getting a kick out of Sophia being so protective over me and I knew Jack would be fine. I snuck up behind them after twenty minutes, I felt as though I had let this go on long enough. I stopped and hid in the hallway, eavesdropping when I realized Sophia was telling Jack about Hannah. She must have been more worried than she let on if she was confiding in a complete stranger, even if it was someone as trusting as Jack.

"Hey guys, how's it going?"
"Beth, I understand what you see in this guy, he's quite the catch."
"Well thank you Sophia, the same could be said about you."

"Now now, break it up," I said in a joking way. "But for real, I overheard you telling him about Hannah. What do you think Jack?"
"If she's anything like Maia, and it sure sounds like she is, I think maybe we give your friend Ethan a call and see if he can help us out."

I had filled Jack in on my conversation with Ethan and agreed that if anyone could help us in finding some information it would probably be him. With Sophia's approval, I called Elizabeth and filled her in on the whole situation.

Ethan did us a favor and pulled some strings with some of his old buddies at the police station. He said they were able to find an address for Hannah Baker but that's all they could give us - even that was pushing it a little but they did it for Ethan. He said his buddies knew he wouldn't be asking for that kind of personal information if it wasn't im-portant. Ethan had made plans to go check out the house the following day.

16

"I'm coming with you."

"No Beth, you're not."

"I already called Elizabeth, she's coming too."

"Definitely not."

"Oh come on. You have to get over your issue with her. She already apologized to you a thousand times Ethan."

"Yes and I appreciated that, but the two of you are not coming with me to check out this house. It's too dangerous, we don't know what we're going to find."

"It might be a dead end."

"And it might not be."

"If you want someone to come with me, send Jack."

"He can't. Sophia is too freaked out and obviously doesn't want to come so Jack offered to stay at the house with her until we got back."

"Well then that's good, you won't be alone while you wait for me to come back. Why don't you tell Elizabeth there's been a change of plans and she can meet you at your house instead and the four of you can wait together for me to come back."

"Ugh fine. You're so annoying."

"I'll call you as soon as I know anything."

I was surprised that Ethan believed me when I said
I would hang back at the house. I didn't even know
what this Hannah person looked like, but maybe
I would soon. I waited for him to drive away then
hurried into my car. I had texted Elizabeth while I
was arguing with Ethan and she was hiding on the
side of the house waiting for me to signal her. She
ran and joined me in the car and we followed Ethan.
He was making so many turns, at first I wasn't sure
if he was lost or if he had seen me in his rear view
mirror and was trying to lose me. I must say, I felt
very accomplished when he pulled up outside of the
house I assume he was looking for. Both Liz and
I watched as he got out and looked at the house,
doing a double take then looking back at the piece
of paper that had the address on it. He scratched his
head as if something was puzzling him then turned
around and got back in his car. I caught up to him
just before he was about to pull away.

"Where do you think you're going?"
"Bethany! What are you doing here? What did I tell
you?"
"You didn't really think I was gonna stay behind did
you?"
"Let me guess your sidekick is back there in the car
too?"
"Correct. So Where are you going? You're not even

gonna knock?”

“There’s no reason to.”

“What? Can you see through walls?”

“What? No. I thought something was familiar about the address and now that I’m here I can confirm my suspicions.”

“About what?”

“My buddies must have made a mistake when they did their research. This can’t be Hannah’s house, this is Gloria’s house.”

“Are you sure?”

“Yes. Where are you going?”

I marched up to that house, before I lost the confidence to do so. As I went, I waved Elizabeth over to come join me. I brought her up to speed, quickly as we neared the front door. Before Ethan could stop me I was banging so hard on that door I could feel the bruises that would show themselves later. To my surprise, it actually was Gloria who opened the door.

“What a nice surprise. What are you ladies doing here? Is that Ethan back there?”

“Hi there Gloria,” we said at the same time.

She invited us in for iced tea and we told her everything. We called Sophia and Jack to invite them
over to meet us, but Jack had to get to work and
Sophia wanted to do her daily meditation. I thought
I should get into that since I always worry so much
about everything - maybe it would help to mellow
me out. I've tried before and was instructed to clear
my mind of all thoughts, but when I did all I could
think about was how I wasn't supposed to think
about anything. The whole thing just made me more
frustrated than anything.

17

I was feeling pretty beat and defeated by the time I got back home. I wanted to leave much earlier than I had, but we all got to talking and ended up staying at Gloria's for most of the afternoon. Jack was busy working so I wouldn't have been able to spend much time with him anyways, but I felt awful about leaving Sophia alone for another day. I was feeling like a terrible friend. She came all this way to see me and we've barely spent any time together. When I got home I was pleasantly surprised to see what was waiting for me. Sophia had rented a movie, ordered pizza, got all our favourite junk foods and candy, and even set up my entire living room into a land of blankets and pillows. It was just like we used to do when we lived together.

"Soph, you didn't have to do all of this."
"I wanted to."
"I should be the one setting all of this up for you, I've been a pretty shitty friend lately."
"Don't you dare. You're the best friend."
"I don't know what I would without you. I wish you didn't live so far away."

"What if I didn't?"
"Omg no way? For real?"
"I've been thinking about it, a lot. There's really no reason I have to stay in Vancouver. I can teach yoga from anywhere. I miss being close to my best friend. Besides, I think you could use a little more family around anyways?"
"Yes but I would never ask you to move across the country for me."
"I know. It was all my idea, and Jack's."
"What! You told Jack before you told me?"
"Well I figured he knows you pretty well, I just wanted to run it by him to see what he thought."
"And?"
"He agreed that it was a great idea. So it's decided, I'm moving to Corner Brook."
"This is the best news I've heard in a long time."

I was so elated that my best friend would be moving here. I know I had Elizabeth, but Sophia was like my sister.

"Well, aren't you gonna call your new BFF and tell her the news?"
"Don't start. But yeah I'll text her."

I texted Liz telling her she would have to officially meet Sophia sooner or later because she was going to be here to stay. All she replied back was "Great. I guess I'll have to get used to having her around." It was kind of weird, it seemed out of character for her, but I didn't care, nothing was going to bring down my mood. Sophia and I spent the night watching movies and stuffing our faces until we felt sick. She must really be worried about me because I haven't seen her eat that much junk food since college. I was surprised she even knew what to buy at the store.

I woke up the next morning in a sea of blankets and realized we must have fallen asleep in the living room. It was eight in the morning, much too early for me but I woke up to a knock on the door.
"I'm coming."
I opened the door to Jack. I was a little mortified that he was seeing me like this, even though I had no reason to be. I just wished I could have at least brushed my teeth first.
"Woah what happened here? He asked as he made his way to the kitchen, stepping over all the pillows in his path.
"Good morning Sophia."
"Hi Jack," she said, lifting a hand out from under a mountain of blankets. If it weren't for the hand you

wouldn't have even known she was there.

"Hey Jack, what's up. I didn't expect to see you so early today - not that I'm complaining."

"I thought we could go for breakfast at the cafe before I meet with Elizabeth."

"Oh right that's today. You're sure I can't stay while you guys talk?"

"Sorry Beth, I'm not changing my mind. I don't want to be swayed by your opinion of her. I want to be able to talk with her alone and form my own opinion to see whether or not I think she would be a good fit for my company."

"Okay fine," I said as I dragged myself up the stairs and into my room to get dressed.

I came back down five minutes later and found Sophia exactly where I had left her and Jack trying his best to tidy up the place without disturbing Sophia. "Oh that's sweet but you don't have to do that. I'll clean up later. Shall we go?"

"Yeah."

This was the earliest I had been at the cafe. I know I said it was different to see it in the daylight when I was here in the afternoon, but the morning was a whole other story. The crowd was so different. There were a lot of families which was nice to see. As we sat down I got a text from Elizabeth telling me how excited she was to finally get to meet Jack. She jokingly assured me that she wasn't sick and didn't for see any work emergencies that would get in the way of them meeting again.

"So what's good here?"
"Jack, you've lived here all your life, are you really going to tell me you've never been in here?"
"No I have. All I ever get is a coffee."
"Of course."

We took a look at the menu, as I actually wasn't sure what was good here as breakfast food. After a lengthy discussion, we both settled on bacon and eggs with a side of fruit - but when the waiter came to take our order I may have also added a side of pancakes. Don't judge me, you would have too if the lady next to you had them and the smell of sweet buttery goodness traveled straight up your nostrils. It was the best decision I made that day - those pancakes were amazing. I ate as slow as I possibly could, but Jack caught on to what I was doing very quick.

"I know exactly what you're doing. Don't even think for a second you can fool me Beth."
"Fool you? What are you talking about?"
"I've seen you eat many things in my lifetime and

never have you eaten that slow."

"I'm just trying to savor it. It's so good. Want a bite?"

Jack leaned over and took the entire half pancake that was left on my plate and shoved the whole thing in his mouth.

"Hey. What did you do that for?"

"So you can go back home and hang out with Sophia while I meet with Elizabeth."

"Oh yeah. I totally forgot about that."

"Sure you did."

"I'll see you later," he said as he leaned over the table one more time - this time to give me a kiss.

"Mmm. You taste like butter."

"Get out of here crazy lady. I'll call you later."

I blew him a kiss and was on my way. I never answered Elizabeth's text from earlier, so I pulled out my phone to let her know we had been at the cafe having breakfast and I was just leaving. She said she was on her way, so I texted Jack to let him know. I thought about texting Sophia, but decided I would just see her in ten minutes when I got home. I had to put my phone away. I don't suggest texting while walking it can be quite dangerous - I almost walked into many things.

***

Now I wasn't actually there for this part, but I'm going to recount it to you the same way I heard jack tell the police.

He said he was sitting at the table in the cafe waiting for Elizabeth to arrive when he heard someone call his name. He turned around expecting to finally put a face to the name but was stunned when he looked right into the eyes of Maia - his ex.

"Maia! What are you doing here? Did you follow me?"

"Oh Jack. You always did think so highly of yourself. Give me a little more credit than that wouldn't you?"

"Don't come any closer to me. Restraining order, remember."

"Don't flatter yourself. Can't a girl just enjoy a cup of coffee in her local cafe?"

"Local? You mean you live here? I thought you moved to Alberta?"

"You can read a whole lot of things on the internet Jack. It doesn't mean they're all true."

"You have to leave or I'll call the police."

"Calm down, I was just leaving."

She sipped the remainder of her coffee and walked out of the cafe not bothering to stop and look back. Jack sat back down in his chair and waited for

Elizabeth to arrive.

Meanwhile, I was at home doing my nails with Sophia. We were kind of horrible at painting them ourselves, but we were saving some money and it was funny. I hobbled over to the counter to check my phone when I heard it go off. The girls in movies always make it look like those foam things you put in between your toes while they're drying are so cute and fun - in reality they're a pain in the ass and they kind of hurt if I'm honest. When I got to my phone, the screen was blinking saying that I had one new message from Elizabeth. I opened it worrying something was wrong but she just said that it was going great and she understood why I liked Jack so much. She said he had gone to the washroom so she hurried and snuck her phone out to give me an update.

It was right about that same time that Jack came into my house. He asked me if I had heard from Liz. I showed him the text messages and he just stood there, placing his hand on his chin - you know the way guys do when they're thinking deeply about something but you don't want to ask them what's wrong because they look so good with their pouty face? I caved and asked him why his face looked like that and that's when he told me that Elizabeth never showed.

"What do you mean she never showed? I have the messages right here saying she was with you half an hour ago."
"I know Beth, I see them, but I can assure you I was in the cafe by myself waiting for her."
"I don't understand."
"Why don't you try calling her and asking her to explain herself. Maybe there was some sort of mix up."
"There must have been."

I called Elizabeth but there was no answer. Then I remembered that there was a barista that worked at the cafe who was also named Jack. Surely she would've known he wasn't the right guy.

"She's not answering, Jack. I think I'm gonna go over to her place and make sure she's alright."
"Beth there's something else I have to tell you."
"Can it wait?"
"Yeah. I'm coming with you. Let's go."

We pulled up to Liz's house and there was a strange car in the driveway I didn't remember seeing the last time I was there. I knocked on the door and was delighted when I heard footsteps coming from inside. When the door opened, it was a strange woman I had never met. She had two toddlers wrapped around each of her legs calling her mom and asking who was the lady at the door. Then from behind I could see a man coming - presumably the woman's husband.

"Oh I'm sorry I didn't mean to bother you, I thought I had the right place but I guess I was wrong."
"Who were you looking for," asked the woman.
"Elizabeth."
"Oh. You have the right place but Elizabeth doesn't live here. Would you like to come in?"

Jack and I followed the family inside their home. I was taken back by what I was seeing. For the most part everything was the same as I remembered it, but all of the pictures had been switched out. Where Elizabeth and her family and friends had been was now replaced by this family - with the pictures that were probably intended to be there from the start. I couldn't understand why she would go through all the trouble to make me believe this was her home.

"What do you mean?"
"We were on vacation. She house sits for us. She's been doing it for a few years now. She usually just

stays here while we're gone. It's easier for her that way and we don't mind. It gives her a nice break from her one bedroom apartment."

"Oh I see." I looked at Jack, letting him know I was entering panic mode again and no longer knew what to say to this woman.

"Is everything alright," she asked me.

"Hi there. I'm Jack. We're friends of Elizabeth. We're new to town and must have misunderstood her. Do you know where we could find her? Do you happen to have her current address?"

"I do, but I'm afraid I don't feel comfortable giving it out to you. I don't mean to be rude, but we just met and I've known Elizabeth for a while now."

"No worries," said Jack. "We understand. Have a nice day, sorry to have bothered you."

"Same to you. No need to apologize it wasn't a bother at all."

"Jack, We have to call Ethan."

18

Do you ever have one of those weird psychic moments when you're about to call someone and your phone starts to ring, and it's them? Please don't tell me it's just me - it can't be. Anyways, I'm getting off topic. Just as Jack and me were about to call Ethan, he called me.

"Woah that was strange, I was just about to call you."

"Really? That is strange, but not as strange as what I'm about to tell you."

"Oh boy. Here we go again. What is it now?"

"You might want to sit down dear."

"Was that Gloria?"

"Yeah, I'm with her right now. I needed another set of eyes to look over what I thought I was seeing to make sure I wasn't losing my mind."

"He wasn't," added Gloria. "You're really gonna want to sit down."

"Can someone please just tell me what's going on? Either of you?"

"Yeah c'mon guys you're even freaking me out a little."

"Oh is that Jack?"

"It's me Gloria, hello."

"You guys! Seriously?"

"Okay," said Ethan. "One of my buddies called me earlier. One of the ones form down at the station. He told me he thought he made a real break in the case this time and that he had some hard evidence on Hannah Baker."

"And?" I said.

"And, he sent me over some documentation. Picture ID, home address and more. But it was the picture ID that threw me off. I couldn't believe what I was seeing.

"You're really starting to scare me Ethan. What did you see?"

"I'm sending it over to you now."

"That can't be right. There must be some kind of mistake like last time when they sent us to Gloria's."

"I'm afraid this is no mistake. It was checked and triple checked. Do you know where Sophia is right now?"

"She should be at home."

"Gloria and me will meet you guys there."

"Let me see the phone Beth," said Jack. "Tell me what's going on."

"I'll show you when we get home, please just drive."

The five minute drive from the house I thought was Elizabeth's back to mine felt like it stretched out for ages. I didn't mean it but I remember being rather rude to Jack, telling him to drive faster even though I knew legally he could not. He took it like a true champ though, not fighting back, knowing he would only be further poking the bear.

"Sophia! Sophia!"
"What are you yelling about?" She was still where Jack and I had left her hours ago, tangled in a pile of blankets. She must have had some sort of junk food hangover.
"I need you to come here right now please and be completely honest with me."
"Alright. Not gonna lie you're kind of freaking me out."
"Please, just do what I'm asking."
"Okay. How come everyone's here? What's going on?"
I ignored her question and opened the door all the way to let Ethan and Gloria into my home. Jack shimmied further away to make room for the other two.
"Can you please come look at the picture on my phone."
"Okay."

Sophia picked up my phone and looked at the photo of Hannah that Ethan had sent me.

"Why do you have that? Where did you find that picture?"

"Do you know who this person is?"

"I mean, the hair and eye colours are different, but that's Hannah."

"You're sure? That's the same girl you told me about the other day?"

"Yes. Why?"

I didn't want to believe what she was telling me. It had to be another misunderstanding like everything had seemed to be lately. But the feeling in the pit of my stomach was telling me that there was too much evidence for this not to be true.

"Beth, what's wrong?"

"The girl in the picture is Elizabeth."

"Are you kidding me right now?"

"I wish I was."

"How did you find this out?"

"Ethan did. His friends from the station found Eliza - Hannah's picture and he sent it to me so I could confirm it with you."

"This is Elizabeth? The girl you've been spending all of your time with?"

When I turned around, Jack had my phone in his hands and he looked as though he had seen a ghost.

"Yes that's her - whoever she is."

"Remember I told you there was something else I had to tell you but that it could wait until later?"

"Yeah."

"I don't think it can wait any later. I said that Elizabeth never showed up at the cafe, but it turns out she did."

"What are you saying?"

"I didn't want to freak you out, I was going to get Ethan's opinion later on what I should do about it all, but when I was waiting in the cafe for Elizabeth, Maia was there."

"What!" Said Sophia who had been filled in on the entire situation by me right after I found out myself.

"Wait," said Jack, "it gets worse."

"I don't see how it possibly could," I said, "but please do go on."

"If you change the cut and colour of the girls hair in that picture, it's Maia."

At that moment I stopped functioning as a human being. My brain didn't know how to process what I was hearing. I was so thankful that I was surrounded by all of my friends and Jack, especially Jack at that moment. It was him who got me to snap out of whatever trance I had been trapped in. I looked around the room, making note of each face that was surrounding me. All I could do was stare at them, hoping one of them would know what to say to make all of this go away.

"So if I have this right, the person I've let into my life and thought was my friend is also your crazy ex roommate and your psychotic ex girlfriend? I didn't think these kind of things actually happened outside of the movies."
"How did you say you met her again," asked Sophia.
"At the train station. She was walking away with my bags so I ran after her. We cleared it up, it was just a mistake - we had the same bag."
"Did you ever see her pick up her own bag?" Asked Gloria.
"Well no. I offered to stay and help her find hers since I knew what it looked like, but she insisted it wasn't necessary so I left. It wasn't until after the first meeting I went to at the support group that I saw her again in the cafe. But it was me who made the first move."
"Maybe that's exactly what she was hoping you would do," said Ethan.
"But how could she have known I would be there?"
"Who knows," said Jack. "Can't you find out an awful lot about a person on the internet now a days? That's why I stay away from all of the social medias for the most part."
"I mean I guess, but I didn't even have her as a

friend until after we met at the cafe."

"Remember what she said when you called her asking if she knew someone by the name of Hannah?" Asked Sophia.

"Not word for word."

"Well I do. She said she would check her socials for you because she accepted almost everyone, including people she didn't know."

"Oh crap."

"I know."

"Can someone please tell me what's going on here," asked Jack.

"We all do it," said Sophia. "We have our privacy settings fairly loose, we accept friend requests from people we've only ever met online. We don't really know anything about them other than what they post."

"For all we know, she could have been following me for a long time and I never would have been aware," I added.

"That is messed up," said Gloria. "What on earth would drive a person to do something so outrageous?"

"I don't know," replied Ethan, "but I'm going to help you find out. Let me make a quick call to my buddies down at the station and fill them in on all of this. They're most likely going to want each of you to go down and explain your individual stories to them."

That's exactly what we all did. We rode in Jack's car, downtown to the police station where we one by one went into the interrogation rooms to provide the officers with every detail we had about Elizabeth, Maia and Hannah. It took so long, each officer had us recount our stories multiple times, asking for more details each time. When we went in, the sun was out and the sky was bright, when we came out it was as if someone flicked a switch, and the sky was black.

Jack dropped Gloria and Ethan off at Gloria's place, he was going to stay with her even though she tried to fight him on it. I had offered for everyone to stay at my place, but there really wasn't that much room. Jack did stay the night though, which made both Sophia and I feel protected.

Hours passed and still there was no word from Elizabeth. As far as we knew she hadn't realized we were on to her, but I really couldn't be sure of anything anymore, considering what she had already gotten away with. The following morning I was woken up by Jack getting out of bed. I followed him down the hall and realized he was going to answer the door. It had taken me so long to fall asleep that by the time I actually had I was in such a deep sleep

I hadn't heard the door bell.

"Wait there Beth."
When I saw Jack welcoming Ethan inside, I pulled Sophia out of bed and went to join the guys downstairs.
"So," I said. "Any news?"
"No leads on where she is right now, but we did find a name - her real name and an address. Turns out the woman you spoke to was telling the truth she lives in a one bedroom apartment. Elizabeth is her middle name. Her real name is Luna."
"Like the moon," asked Jack?
"Omg she was messing with me the entire time."
"What do you mean Beth?" Asked Sophia.
"Jack do you remember our first date, at the movies?"
"Of course I do."
"The necklace I was wearing. It was a crescent moon. It was hers, she insisted that I wear it because it tied the outfit together."
"Maia always did have a strange fascination with the moon. I never would have put two and two together."
"By the way, Ethan. I've been meaning to ask you about something."
"I have a feeling I know where this is going," he said.

"Were you at the movies the night I was there with Jack?"

"I thought you wanted me there. When I realized I was wrong, I left right away."

"That's why I couldn't find you. I don't mean to sound rude, but what would have given you the impression I wanted you to come to the movies with Jack and me?"

"You texted me."

"No I didn't,"

"You did. You told me which theatre, which movie and which time. I thought it was a cryptic invitation, like a fun new friend game."

"I can't believe this."

"What I was only joking."

"No. Not you. Eliza- Luna was helping me get ready for my date with Jack, I borrowed an outfit from her. I had forgot all of my things at her place and she brought them back to me hours later. She had my phone with her for hours giving her more than enough time to send you that text. It was all part of her plan to make me question you. She made you out to be some creep so I would forget about the feeling you were having towards her. I'm so sorry Ethan, I should have believed you. You were right the whole time."

"There's no need to apologize, it won't do us any good. Let's just think back to everything we know about this person so we can track her down and figure out why she's doing all of this."

19

"Ethan, did you say your friend gave you an address for Hannah Baker?"

"Yeah, but I don't think -"

"Well what are we still doing here," said Gloria.

"I swung by there before I went to Gloria's house, and I'm just not sure that we should go over there right now."

"Why not," I said. "We might see something that can help us find her."

"That's what I'm afraid of," Ethan muttered under his breath.

Against his opinion, Ethan finally caved and agreed to bring us to the address he was given. We still were unsure of whether or not she knew we were on to her, but we didn't think she would be at her place. She still never called me back, so she must have at least known something was up. We arrived to a run down apartment building in a part of town I was not familiar with. The area gave me the creeps, it looked like a ghost town. There was no one and nothing in sight besides the building that was in shambles. Ethan and Jack went in first - there wasn't much room for all of us so the girls waited in the hall. We didn't have much trouble getting in as the front door of the building was not protected and the apartment door was unlocked. I guess she never thought anyone would find this place. Jack came out of the one bedroom and looked spooked. I've known Jack most of my life and I already told you about his love for horror films, I've never seen anything scare Jack before so I knew I should prepare myself.

"I think maybe we should just go home," said Jack. "Nothing in there is going to help us find her."
"But we're already here," I said. "It can't be that -"

Bad is the word I was about to say, but stopped myself when I saw the contents of the room. It was filled with week old take out containers that were being swarmed by flies, empty wrappers and dishes piled so high I was amazed they hadn't come crashing down with a bang. That wasn't even the worst of it. At first I thought it was some sort of eclectic wallpaper print, but when I got closer I saw that it was all pictures of me and my life. There were some of Jack that went back to the time he was in high school - I could tell by the length of his hair. There were pictures of Sophia in her dorm room, taken from an angle that made it clear she wasn't aware she was being photographed.

She had dedicated an entire section of the wall where she cut out her head and glued it on top of mine in pictures of me out with friends and family, with Jack and even some of my selfies from instagram that dated back to my college days.

"Why would she do all of this," I questioned out loud to anyone who wanted to try answer. "I just met this girl a few weeks ago."
"Well it seems she's been aware of you for a lot longer than that," said Sophia.
"Are you sure you don't know her from anywhere?"
"No Sophia. I think I would have remembered when I saw her that first day in the train station. How could she have known I would be there?"
"I don't know."

I stopped listening to what everyone was saying when something caught my attention from the corner of my eye. I walked right up to the section of the wall where the picture was, leaving only a few inches of breathing room between the wall and myself. I wanted to be sure I was seeing clearly.

"Jack, come over here. You need to see this."
"Woah. Is that?"
"My parents."

"But who's that other woman?"
"I have no idea. I've never seen her before."

I pulled the picture of my parents and me off of the wall. I must have been about sixteen years old because I still had my braces on. I don't think I ever posted this picture anywhere, how could she have gotten it.

"Maybe you should call your parents," said Sophia.
"Maybe you're right."

***

"Mom?"
"Hey honey, it's so nice to hear from you. How are things? Are you settling in okay? We'll have to come by and visit once you're settled."
"Is dad home?"
"Is something wrong?"
"I'm not sure. Can you please put dad on the phone?"
"Sure. Love you."
"Love you too mom."

"Hey there Beth, is everything alright?"
"Hey dad, yeah everything is fine I just had a question I thought you might be able to help me out

with."

"What is it?"

"I was going through some old pictures and I came across one of you and a woman that I've never seen before."

"What did she look like?"

"Tall, long dark hair and I think she may have been pregnant."

"That must be Isabelle, Izzy."

"Who's Izzy?"

"She was my girlfriend just before I met your mother. Things didn't end very well with her and I, I'm surprised that picture is still around it must have gotten mixed up in your things you can toss it out."

"But dad, she looked pregnant in the picture."

"She was."

"You have another kid you never told me about?"

"No no. She lost the baby just before we split up."

"You dumped her because she lost your child?"

"No sweetheart. Things had been going down hill far before I even learned she was pregnant. She was troubled. Always had been. She said I was abandoning her and the stress of it caused her to lose the baby."

"How come you never told me any of this before?"

"Your mother and I never thought it was necessary, she's been out of my life for a long time."

"Oh okay. Thanks dad. Hey I gotta get going, say

bye to mom for me."

"Sure thing kiddo. Talk soon."

"Did anyone hear that?"

"I did," said Gloria, looking a little too excited considering the circumstance. "Let me get this straight. Your father has a secret love child or should I say hate child with a crazy or troubled lady as he put it and he seems to have no idea the kid exists."

"And Luna is that child," asked Sophia.

"It's really looking that way. I just don't understand how she knew where I would be."

"Are you really that stupid? For someone who otherwise seems so smart, you sure do put an awful lot of personal information online. You look confused. Let me refresh your memory. Do you recall changing your place of living from Vancouver to Corner Brook then checking in once your train pulled into the station?"

We all spun around at the sound of another voice that didn't belong to any of us. There she was , Luna, seemingly appearing out of nowhere, making her way into the room from the darkness of the hallway. I knew I was looking at the same person I had spent almost all of my time with these past few days, but something about her was different. The look in her eyes was so sinister. She walked right up to us as if it was where she felt she belonged. She must have been delusional thinking she was actually part of this group.

"What is wrong with you," I screamed as I lunged forward. I didn't get very far when Jack's arm interfered between Luna and me, pulling me towards him.

"Bethany stop," he said.

"Let me go. She's going to get away."

"This isn't the way to handle things."

I could see in her eyes that she was loving how Jack was protecting her. It was just making me more angry and I forced all of my weight against his trying to break free of his hold. Just as I was about to get loose and lunge for her again, Sophia tripped me. This had to be some kind of sick joke. All of my friends were clearly defending this crazy bitch who messed with each one of their lives. I was about to lose my mind when I looked over at Ethan. He had managed to get around all of us and was standing in the doorway. He sneakily placed a large rope that he had tied in a loop around Luna's arms and pulled it tight while Jack had her distracted. Ethan just kept amazing me with all of his hidden talents. The way he wrangled her up in that rope, I wouldn't be surprised if he told me he used to work on a ranch or participate in the rodeo. Jack reached out and gave my shoulders a little squeeze and Sophia winked at me, letting me know they were just going along with Ethan's plan to distract Luna - I felt myself begin to call down. I will admit, I'm not proud of how we handled things, we should have taken her to the police right away and let them handle it, but I needed answers and I needed to hear them from her.

20

"You know you can't hold me here against my will. It's illegal."

"Do you really want to go there right now," I asked. That seemed to shut her up real quick. At least she knew what she was doing was wrong.

"I just have one question for you, whoever you really are. What did I ever do to you that made you hate me so much? I don't even know you."

"You stole my life from me. Don't you get it? Everything you have should have been mine."

"What does that even mean? I just met you the other day."

"But I've known you for a long time. I'll never forget the day I met you. The day I saw how my life was supposed to turn out until you stole it."

"You're crazy. I've never met you before the train station."

"That's what you think. Why don't you call daddy and ask?"

I knew she had to be messing with me but I couldn't help but squirm. I knew she could sense how uncomfortable she was making me. The fact that she managed to maneuver her way into my life so easily and I just let her.

"So what's it going to be? Are you gonna call daddy or do you wanna hear it from me first?"
"Why should I believe anything you say?"
"Because I'm your sister."
"You are not. Do not call me that."
"Fine. You never were any good at it anyways."
"You are insane. You were never really sick were you? And I bet it was you watching Jack and me on our date. No one else knew we would be at the theatre."
"Bravo, you catch on quick. I guess genius runs in the family."
The way she said family made me want to hurl. She let the letters linger for a moment too long making a normally heart warming word sound so haunting.
"What about Luke? Did you ever have a husband?"
"What do you think?"

I just stared at her waiting for her to continue.
"I didn't have a husband, but my heart was broken - by him."
She hissed out those last few words and glared right at Jack.
"So all of this is because Jack didn't feel the same way you felt about him?"
"No. It's about you. Have you not been listening

to a thing I've been saying. You have everything that should be mine. The family, the best friend and the boys."

"Why did you say boys as if there were more than one?"

"Let's just say Aiden didn't fall that day at work."

Hearing his name come out of her mouth really pushed me over the edge. My ears started to ring and I began to lose my balance. The next thing I knew I was looking up at Jack from on the floor. He helped me up and was saying something but I wasn't listening to him. I was distracted by what Luna was saying.

"It's just so easy with you, You really do believe anything I say. I read about Aiden in the paper. You can find a lot of things in there. For example the tragic story of how a young wife lost her husband on a dark highway."

"That necklace."

"What," I said, pausing a moment to allow my voice to return back to normal once it registered that it was Jack who was now speaking."

"It didn't click with me before, but that necklace, the one you were wearing on our date Beth."

"What about it?"

"It was a gift for Maia from one of those machines at the arcades. We got it on our first date. She always had a thing for the moon and the stars."
"I knew you would remember," said Luna. "I knew you still cared."
"Think again crazy lady. He didn't care for you then in that way and he sure as hell does not now. And while we're telling truths, you were the worst roommate I ever had and you didn't even come close to being Bethany so you might as well just drop the act right now and go back to crazy town," said Sophia.
"Oh I'll leave. But I will be back. I always come back. I've been following you since you turned sixteen Bethany. The same day as my eighteenth birthday when I was finally old enough to learn the truth. I found my birth father, the one who abandoned me before I was even born. I had to see who his new family was. The one he felt was so much better than what he had with my mom. I never could figure out what it was."
"My father doesn't even know you exist."
"Are you sure about that?"

I knew she was still just trying to get in my head and further mess with me, but it was kind of working. Everyone was staring at me waiting for me to make the next move.

"I'm calling him. Is that what you want? Are you happy now?"

She just sat there with a smug look on her face, taunting me without even saying a word.

"Bethany?"

"Hi Dad."

"Can you see me?"

"No Dad. Tilt the phone up towards your face please."

"Better?"

"It'll do. Look Dad I have a sort of strange question to ask you. Do you know this woman?" I flipped the camera so that it was now facing Luna, making sure to get her from the shoulders up so he couldn't see that she was tied to the chair.

"Oh honey come quick Beth is with Luna, what a small world."

"Luna, I haven't heard that name in ages," called my mom from somewhere in the background.

"How did you two meet," asked dad.

"You know her?"

"Of course. She used to work at the diner your mom and me always went to. She was our waitress the very first time we went in and we got to know her so every time after that we called ahead to make sure there as a table available in her section."

"How come I never met her?"

"I'm not sure honey, maybe she wasn't in the few times you came to the diner with us."

"What a strange coincidence," said Luna in a voice that made her seem so innocent.

"It's so nice to see you dear," said mom. "Are you still working at the diner?"

"Oh no those days are long gone."

"How did you two meet?"

Luna jumped in before I had the time to stop her. "It's a funny story actually. I grabbed her bag by mistake at the train station and we just hit it off. When I saw her last name I had to ask if she was your daughter. I remembered you guys telling me you had a daughter but I wanted to be sure. It really is such a small world."

"That's wonderful," said dad. "We'll all have to get together one day for old times sake."

"I would love that," said Luna.

"Yeah sure dad. Sounds great. We have to go. I'll talk to you guys soon."

I hung up the phone before they had the chance to make any more plans that were never going to happen. I was at a loss for words once again and it didn't seem as though any of my friends were ready to step in.

"I made him love me."

"What," I asked.

"Dad. He got to know me and loved me just like you do."

"I do not love you. You are not at all the person I have been spending all of my time with. None of it was real. You know maybe you actually could have had a family in us if you didn't ruin it."

"That's not true and you know it. So I did the only thing I could. I wanted your heart to hurt as much as mine did. It was just so unfair, you know? My mother never wanted me. She overdosed a few days after I was born. I was all alone in the world - until I found you. I bounced around foster homes my entire childhood. Some weren't so bad - but they weren't my family. I didn't always want to hurt you. You have to believe me. I loved you - but then I found out the truth. He isn't even your real father. I had to find out what made him choose you over me- his own blood. I had no choice but to become you."

Ethan and Gloria had completely removed themselves from the situation and were now looking at all of the images that covered the walls. Jack and Sophia were close by, but they were waiting for me to say something first. My mind was racing so fast and I only looked away from Luna for a brief moment - a brief moment too long. It all happened at once. I was yelling for Jack and Ethan to grab her and put her back in the chair. Somehow she had managed to wriggle herself free of the ropes that had her arms pinned down along her sides. Everyone ran at her in the same moment and we all collided, giving her just enough time to get away. She ran down he stairs of the apartment building and out into the street. What happened next is still a little bit of a blur - maybe because of how fast it all happened or maybe because my mind tried to block it out of my memories.

This wasn't at all what I hoped would come of this. There wasn't any way any one of us could have stopped the truck, it was coming so quickly and Luna was in such a rush to get away she mustn't have looked. The police and paramedics came rushing to the scene, sirens blaring from miles away, but they were too late. "She came out of nowhere," I remember the truck driver yelling repeatedly - seems I wasn't the only one who was traumatized by the incident. When I managed to calm down slightly, I called my parents once again and explained everything to them. My dad was devastated. It turned out Luna was lying and he really did have no idea who she was. We all attended her funeral a week later, and were sadly the only ones there. My parents and I, Jack, Sophia, Ethan and Gloria all stood in a line afraid to move or say the wrong thing. I hated to admit, it made me feel like a horrible human being, but a part of me felt the tiniest bit of relief that she was gone. I went home that night and deleted all of my social media accounts. I wasn't taking any chances. Besides everything I needed was right here with me. I used to rely so much on the world inside of my phone screen - it was freeing to say goodbye.

21

It had been six months since the day Luna left. Sometimes when I was out alone, I swore I saw her crossing the street on the opposite side, or sitting in the cafe sipping a latte and eating a brownie. I had let her in and gotten so used to having her around in a matter of days, but it was taking so long to rid her from my memories. Sometimes, although only for a few seconds at a time, I missed the friend I had in Elizabeth. I know it was all fake and she did all of the right things to make sure we got along perfectly. She made sure I got attached to her so it would hurt all that much more when she disappeared. I wonder if some part of her felt remorse for what she did. She spent so much of her life trying to ruin mine that she missed out on the one she could have had.

 I hadn't stepped foot back inside that cafe since I had been with Elizabeth, but today was different - I was ready to move on. I was running late, it was half past twelve and I should have been there at noon. I was meeting Jack for my birthday, we were going to have a low key lunch and go home and watch movies.

"SURPRISE!"

I looked around the cafe, smiling joining into the surprise chants, wondering who the lucky person was - then I realized it was me. The whole cafe was decorated with balloons and banners. The very best part was my friends, all of them right in the middle of the cafe. There was Sophia, Gloria, Ethan and Jack - oh Jack he did all of this for me and I had no idea. I often asked myself what on earth I did to deserve him. I thought I had already had my one chance at true love, but it seems I lucked out in that department. For just a second when I looked back at the table I saw Aiden. He was standing in the back, out of sight looking over everyone. I still haven't gotten used to my birthday without him and I was worried he wasn't going to show up.

"Hey," said Jack, "are you alright? You're not mad are you?"
"No of course not. This is great. Everyone I love is here."

We spent the rest of the afternoon eating cake and laughing. Sophia was more than ready to keep the party going but it was getting late and a relaxing night at home was more my speed these days. Jack and me said our goodbyes to our friends and went back home to the house that he had built for us. He surprised me with it about a month ago. It was beautiful and everything I could have ever imagined.

"Thank you for the best birthday."
"You're more than welcome. I thought you would want to go all out this year since we'll have our hands full next year."
"You're the best."
"Do you think we can tell everyone soon?"
"I think so."

The following weekend, we had all of our friends over to the house to make our big announcement - turned out we weren't the only ones with exciting news. Ethan and Sophia arrived together, and we were just waiting on Gloria.

"Hey Soph - wait - are you guys holding hands?" Ethan and Sophia smiled and lifted their hands up so I could see how their fingers were perfectly intertwined.
"Omg that's great. Wait Ethan, I thought-"
"You love who you love," said Ethan.
"We wanted to wait to tell you guys," said Sophia.
"We didn't want to steal your thunder at your birthday party."
"No way, congratulations you guys," said Jack who just joined all of us in the doorway. "Come in come

in."
As we were ushering everyone inside, Gloria came running from down the road. "Wait for me," she hollered.

We wanted to wait until the end of the night to tell everyone our news, but when Gloria and Sophia got into the wine, I knew we would have to change our plans. We had this whole speech planned out but like I've learned, things don't always go as planned but that's okay.

"Here Beth," said Sophia as she handed me a glass of wine."
"Unless that's grape juice, I'll be taking that," said Jack as he came and took the wine glass out of my hands with a smile on his face.

"No way," said Gloria and she covered her mouth and tears welled up in her eyes.
"Yes way I said," placing my hands over my tiny bump. "We're having a baby."
"Oh congratulations you guys, we're all so happy for you. Gosh look at me I'm a complete mess."

We all laughed and surrounded Gloria in a giant friend group hug.

The following year was a whirlwind of amazing things. So much happened in such a sort amount of time, but I wouldn't have wanted it any other way. Jack and I got married after we welcomed our beautiful daughter Sawyer who watched us get married with her aunt Sophia and uncle Ethan - who were also engaged might I add. It wasn't a big giant wedding like I always thought I wanted, but it was perfect. We had it at Jack's parent's house in the front yard - the porch swing being the center piece of the whole evening. My parents were there, Gloria was there and that was all. We wanted to have a small intimate ceremony with the important people in our lives. Sophia was my maid of honor and Ethan was Jack's best man - they spent a lot of time together doing guy things after everything cleared up and they realized they really enjoyed each others company. This was great news for Sophia and I as it gave us plenty of time to do our girly things and have a break from the boys. Don't get me wrong, we love them but some things are meant just for girlfriends.

Gloria was ready to head out on a cruise with some of her friends from her art classes. I never actually made it down to one of those, but I promised her I would make it to one when she got back from her trip. There was no rush now since Sophia was here to stay. I couldn't wait for her to get back so I could see all of the wild things I knew she would do. She had really taught me not to take everything so seriously and I appreciated her for that.

Sophia and Ethan had plans to move in together and they asked Jack to build their house for them. I was even going to be returning to work just as soon as I was ready to leave Sawyer. Recent events had really opened up all of our eyes to the reality that life is short and very unexpected. It's important to do what makes you happy with the people you love when it feels right. You can never be certain of what the future holds so always live in the moment and be present. We had no idea what was in store for any of us, but we could be certain that we were going to love every minute of it.

Cover Design by Chelsea Robillard
www.chelsearobillard.com
instagram: c_rdesigns

Opening quote:
https://www.nme.com/photos/jack-white-26-quotes-that-will-make-you-stop-
and-think-1416474